When Dance The Moons

☽ ● ☾

Prenellium City Chronicles—Book 1

Karen Toots

Order this book online at www.trafford.com/08-0834
or email orders@trafford.com

Most Trafford titles are also available at major online book retailers.

Note for Librarians: A cataloguing record for this book is available from Library
and Archives Canada at www.collectionscanada.ca/amicus/index-e.html

Printed in Victoria, BC, Canada.

ISBN: 978-1-4251-5675-6 (soft)
ISBN: 978-1-4251-7161-2 (ebook)

*We at Trafford believe that it is the responsibility of us all, as both individuals and corporations,
to make choices that are environmentally and socially sound. You, in turn, are supporting this
responsible conduct each time you purchase a Trafford book, or make use of our publishing services.
To find out how you are helping, please visit www.trafford.com/responsiblepublishing.html*

*Our mission is to efficiently provide the world's finest, most comprehensive book publishing
service, enabling every author to experience success. To find out how to publish your book, your
way, and have it available worldwide, visit us online at www.trafford.com/10510*

Trafford rev. 5/28/2009

Trafford
PUBLISHING®   www.trafford.com

North America & international
toll-free: 1 888 232 4444 (USA & Canada)
phone: 250 383 6864 ♦ fax: 250 383 6804 ♦ email: info@trafford.com

The United Kingdom & Europe
phone: +44 (0)1865 487 395 ♦ local rate: 0845 230 9601
facsimile: +44 (0)1865 481 507 ♦ email: info.uk@trafford.com

10 9 8 7 6 5 4 3 2 1

Dedication:

For my husband Richard, without whose support and encouragement
this book would not have been possible. In fact, he has helped
so much with proofreading, and brainstorming ideas when I hit
a snag, that he should almost be considered as a co-author.

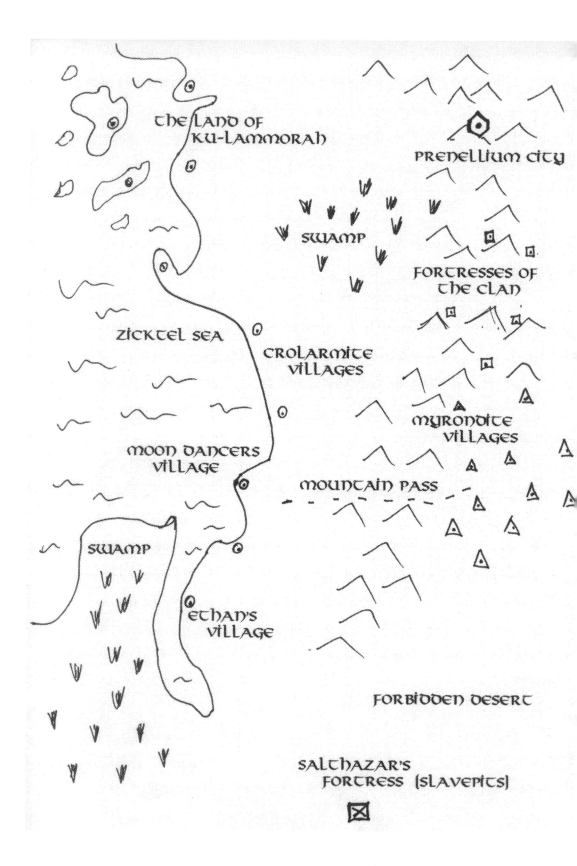

THE LAND OF
KU-LAMMORAH

PRENELLIUM CITY

SWAMP

FORTRESSES OF
THE CLAN

ZICKTEL SEA

CROLARMITE
VILLAGES

MYRONDITE
VILLAGES

MOON DANCERS
VILLAGE

MOUNTAIN PASS

SWAMP

ETHAN'S
VILLAGE

FORBIDDEN DESERT

SALTHAZAR'S
FORTRESS (SLAVEPITS)

Prologue:

Afternoon sunlight poured through the round window into the small cluttered cottage. Among the piles of ancient books and scrolls sat an old man, deep in thought. Old Greplog paused, staring at the ceiling as if seeking wisdom. Worry had etched deep furrows in his forehead. Shaking his gray head, he muttered to himself.

"How can it be? I see rivers of blood. I see famine, disease and death. I feel some ancient evil awakening to threaten us all. So many prophesies. All of them pointing to this year for the fulfillment of these things. But wait, yes I see an even greater good. What does it all mean? It is certain that these will be perilous times if we do not dance the moons...." He briefly shuffled papers around until he found the one he was looking for. Holding it up to the light he read aloud. "When the three moons in harvest full in sacred triangle stand; then dance the dance and pay their due lest tragedy stalk the land... We cannot allow anything to prevent us holding the moon festival. May the High King have mercy on us." Greplog bowed his head in prayer.

About the Author:

Karen Toots loves books and has been a bookworm since she was a small child. She has been writing for many years, but "When dance the moons" is the first book she has had published. She has several more writing projects in the works, including the sequel to "When dance the moons" titled "Out of the Purple Deep".

Karen currently lives in Aldergrove. B.C. with her husband Richard and her two dogs Betsy (a Border collie / Springer spaniel cross) and Billy (a Golden retriever / Australian shepherd cross)

Moon Dancers

☽ ● ☾

Chapter one:

THE MORNING SUNSHINE filtered through the leaves of the tall wide spreading gumphalas trees, filling the small forest glade with a warm, golden glow. Five attractive girls dipped and twirled as they danced around in a circle. Thirteen-year-old Nordelia, slightly smaller and younger than the five dancers, sat watching nearby. She leaned back against the trunk of the tree behind her, absently winding a strand of her sandy blonde hair around one of her fingers. One of the five dancers, her chestnut curls bobbing up and down as she danced, was her best friend Resha. Resha flashed a quick grin as her laughing brown eyes met Nordelia's. The answering smile on Nordelia's freckled face could not hide the wistful expression in her lovely violet eyes. She pushed her straight, sandy blonde hair off her face, as blissfully unaware as the dancers that she was not the only one observing. From behind a nearby tree, two shadowy figures peered intently at the scene before them in the little clearing.

"Not yet." The first one spoke in an undertone, placing a restraining hand on his companion's sleeve. "We are to capture the others first, then the five moon dancers." The two then melted into the forest leaving no sign that they had been there.

The entire village was in darkness. It was very late. Even the communal fire in the village square had gone out. "Good!" thought sixteen year old Shimar, as she crept out of the house. "Everyone must be asleep." She just had to talk to Jonkin. She had not seen or talked to her betrothed for three days. Curse the moon festival! She had been too busy to check on him. Against propriety, she decided to go to his small cottage on the outskirts of the village and find out what was wrong. What if he is ill? Surely someone else in the village would have known and told her if this were the case. Perhaps he was sulking because he was feeling ignored or neglected. However, that wasn't like Jonkin either. By the moons! What in the name of the Prenellium city was up with him?

Shimar had so much on her mind that she scarcely noticed how brightly the stars twinkled overhead, while her long legs rapidly took her through the village. The three moons of Ku-lamorrah would be full and in the position of the sacred triangle on 15th day of Quatsiyr, when Shimar's people, the Crolarmites held the annual moon festival. It was rare for the moons to be in this sacred position, especially in conjunction with the harvest full moons. There was some controversy in the village as to whether this boded good or ill luck, though most agreed that it was a good sign. It was her village's turn to host the festival, therefore the dancers were also chosen from her village. Shimar was one of the five girls picked to be a moon dancer. Quite an honor. Especially this year that promised to be so special. A gentle sea breeze played with her long, smooth brown hair as she made her way quietly along the beach. There was no need for a lantern because her way was lit by the soft glow from the phosphorescent brineconc seaweed that lay strewn along the shore of the Zicktel Sea.

When she reached Jonkin's house she was not at all surprised that no lights were on, but she was alarmed to find the front door wide open. She entered and called out, but there was no response. A cold shiver went down Shimar's back as her limpid blue eyes swept the shadowy room, resting on the cold ashes in the fireplace. No one was home. By all appearances, no one had been here all day. She could see no signs of a struggle. In her mind, she could clearly picture Jonkin, his thick, sandy blonde hair framing his freckled face. She could hear his warm laughter and see his boyish grin and smiling hazel eyes. What in the name of the Prenellium City had happened to him? Silently she turned and left the cabin, her heart and mind tumbling in confusion.

Shimar wandered aimlessly along the seashore for a bit, and then found herself heading inland towards the foothills. She needed some time to think, to sort all this out. Was there a connection between Jonkin's disappearance and the rumors that Myrondites had been spotted in the area? It seemed likely. If Myrondites were skulking about, then what were they up to? Shimar trembled with fear at the stories she had heard about these desert bandits and their bloodthirsty ways. In fact, she had heard that they literally drank blood as part of their strange religion. Such thoughts caused her to question the wisdom of being away from the village by herself in the middle of the night. She succeeded so well in frightening herself, that she was about to scurry back home, when she smelled the smoke of a campfire and heard the murmur of voices coming from the other side of a hill. Taking the rumors into account she felt sure it had to be Myrondites. Who else would be out here at this unholy hour? She had to know for sure so that she could warn her village. Shimar felt the cold, clammy hand of fear clutch her heart as she crept up the side of the hill, and hid behind an outcropping of rocks at the top of the rise.

Cautiously she peeked down into the hollow where the campfire was. To her immense relief she realized immediately that it was not Myrondites. But the group of men gathered below included all the troublemakers and lowlifes of her village. She was relieved to see that her beloved Jonkin was not in such company. Where on Ku-lammorah could he be? Just what were these thugs up to having a secret meeting in the middle of the night? Not anything good, that much was certain.

Draklog, the speaker, was a great bear of a man, with fiery red hair and a temper to match. He was loud and bossy and most of the men in the village had a healthy respect for his powerful fists. Whatever it was about, it was clear to Shimar that they would not be pleased to discover her spying on them.

"We have got to get the Myrondites out of the way!" Draklog declared vehemently. "I will not have those disgusting barbarians interfering with our plans!" Shimar didn't like the Myrondites, and was more than a little afraid of them, but the raw hatred in Draklog's voice made her shudder.

"If they were to get blamed for something really bad then perhaps the elders would agree to go to war against them." commented a rather greasy looking little man with a sharp nose and a pointed chin. Shimar recognized him as Eliphaz, one of her least favorite people.

"Hm-m-m-m" Draklog pondered. "That might have possibilities. However, what would be catastrophic enough to spur the elders into action? You know how difficult it is to get those old weaklings to do anything."

"Perhaps we could pin the blame on the Myrondites for the disappearance of young Jonkin." Eliphaz suggested.

"I somehow doubt that that would do it!" Draklog shook his massive head slowly from side to side. "Besides, how could we get it blamed on the Myrondites? The elders would want proof."

"Then we give them proof. Even if it means manufacturing it." Eliphaz said with a sickening laugh. "The stories we started about seeing Myrondites sneaking around should help."

"Perhaps, but it won't be easy to convince them. They probably suspect, as we do, that Jonkin merely decided to journey, like so many young men do, and wished to avoid all the fuss of good byes."

Shimar was filled with outrage. How dare he suggest such a thing! Jonkin would not just leave like that. Especially now, just before the Moon festival. Moreover, he most definitely would not have left without saying good-bye. The evening was warm, but Shimar felt a chill as she realized what this meant. If her love had not left willingly, then he must have been taken against his will. On the other hand, perhaps some accident had befallen him, and he was lying hurt somewhere. Shimar could not shake the feeling that Jonkin was in grave danger and needed help. Draklog's booming voice drew her attention back to the conversation around the campfire.

"Lord Salthazar will not be pleased by further delays. We must act quickly or risk his wrath."

"You are right as always," agreed Eliphaz in a flattering tone. "I, for one, have no desire to face Lord Salthazar when he is displeased. The problem remains how to go about instigating this war with the Myrondites."

Shimar couldn't make out anything from the hubbub that followed as everyone tried to talk at once. Presently the voices died down and it looked as if the meeting was about to break up. Shimar didn't know what, if anything, had been decided, but fear of being discovered sent her scurrying back to the village as swiftly as her long legs would take her. Her mind whirled around in circles trying to make some sense of the things, she had heard. She had so many questions that she didn't know how to find the answers to. What had become of Jonkin? Exactly what were Draklog and his bunch up to? And why? What in the name of the Prenellium City does Lord Salthazar have to do with all of this? Why would he wish a war between her people and the Myrondites? And why would Draklog and his fellow conspirators wish to help him? Shimar knew very little about Lord Salthazar except that he was a very powerful ruler who had his kingdom in the southern desert. Her people paid a tribute to him each year. She suspected this was largely due to fear of his huge army of Tephanite soldiers. Perhaps some, like Draklog, were a little more serious in their service.

Shimar couldn't shake a feeling of urgency. She must do something. But what? Who could she tell? Who would listen and take her concerns seriously? Draklog was right about one thing. It would do no good to notify the elders. They would do nothing. No! It was up to her.

First, she would check and make sure that Jonkin was not a prisoner of the Myrondites. There were a number of Myrondite villages just on the other side of the coastal range. It was not a terribly long journey through the mountain pass. With any luck, she could be back before the festival. Although she took her role as moon dancer very seriously, she could not rest until she had discovered what had become of her love.

Arriving home, Shimar entered her cottage as quietly as possible in order to avoid waking her family. Fumbling in the dark, she located and put on her warm winter wrap, fastening it securely in place. The thought of traveling alone and unarmed into the very lair of the dreaded Myrondites caused her stomach to knot with fear. She refused to allow herself to dwell on such thoughts, for if she did she was almost certain to change her mind about going. She hated to leave without telling anyone, but she knew it was necessary, since there was no way she would be given permission. It felt good to be doing something.

She pushed aside her apprehension, as well as a twinge of guilt, as she gathered a few provisions and the blanket from her bed, and put them in her pack. Pausing to take a deep breath in order to build up her courage, she slipped quietly out of the house. The first silver fingers of dawn were just starting to appear, crowning the coastal mountains. Without looking back, she headed east with large purposeful strides. She would just have to return as quickly as possible and face whatever consequences awaited.

In the bright morning sunlight, fourteen-year-old Tonash ran along the shores of the Zicktel Sea, tightly clutching a package to her chest. Her father Urilos had gone to the dock earlier to ready the small fishing boat, and she was bringing him his lunch. The package that she carried contained lunch for two people. With her older brother, Pakstrig, at home sick, Tonash was confident that she could convince her father to take her along. She had been out in the fishing boat with her father and brother a number of times, so she knew the basics of operating the small craft. She loved it out on the open sea, and this time it would be just her and her father. Tonash adored Urilos and the thought of spending the whole day out in the boat with him filled her with even more pleasure than when she had been chosen to be one of the five moon dancers at the up coming festival.

Green waves rolled onto the beach and a stiff breeze sent Tonash's dark curls flying out behind her as she raced along the beach to the dock where her father had his boat moored. Contrary to the normal morning hustle and bustle, the docks were quiet and deserted.

"Oh dear, it must be even later than I thought." Tonash muttered to herself. "It looks like all the other boats have left already. I do hope father won't be angry at being kept waiting."

In less then a minute she had reached her fathers boat, the only one still tied to the dock. There was no sign of Urilos anywhere about. She shielded her eyes from the morning sun as she gazed down the beach, hoping to spot her father's familiar figure, but there was not a soul in sight. She turned and looked back the way she had come, still there was no one. The only sounds she could hear were the waves lapping on the shore and the lonely cry of a sea bird.

Even if he had not guessed how much she wanted to go with him, he knew that she would be bringing him his lunch. Why had he not waited for her?

Tonash examined the boat and the area around it for clues. The only thing she found were two pairs of footprints leading to the wooden dock and ending there. She was quite sure one set of footprints belonged to her father, but the others not only dwarfed Tonash's dainty feet, but were significantly larger then the marks made by Urilos' feet. She could think of only one person in the village who possessed such large feet. Draklog! Tonash found his fierce manner frightening. He was so big and bad tempered, and those piercing green eyes of his seem to look right through you. She knew her father would not choose to go out in Draklog's boat. Besides, Draklog had three strong sons to help him, so it was unlikely that he would take anyone else along. Every fiber of Tonash's being told her that something was dreadfully wrong, that her father was in some kind of danger. What should she do? Concern clouded her lovely blue eyes, and her forehead wrinkled into a worried frown.

Fifteen-year-old Cleotisha tossed her wild mane of red hair impatiently, anger smoldering in her snappy green eyes. By the moons! What was taking grandma Wenoch so long at the spring? It had been almost an hour since she had left to fetch the water. She must have run into a couple of her old cronies, and they are standing around gossiping, Cleotisha thought with annoyance.

"I have got to get supper ready and I need that water to cook these vegetables! Father will be home soon, and if supper is late, he will be angry. Neither he nor my brothers show any appreciation for all the work I do around here, but let dinner be a few minutes late, and boy do I hear about it!" Cleotisha grumbled aloud to no one in particular. Finally, with a sigh of resignation, she slammed down the knife that she had been using to chop the vegetables, and headed out the door to the spring.

The street was deserted. The position of the sun, as well as the smells of cooking coming from the other cottages, informed Cleotisha that it was even later than she has supposed. She broke into a run, and arrived at the spring a few moments later. That was odd! There was no one here either. Her calls were greeted only by the ominous silence that permeated the sheltered glade that surrounded the spring.

Everyone must be at home either cooking or already eating their supper. But where could grandma Wenoch be? Just then Cleotisha spotted an over turned water jug abandoned near by. That was strange. Why would anyone leave their jug behind?

As she bent to retrieve it, a feeling of dread filled her. There could be no mistake. It was her grandmother's jug. She called again. And again, there was no reply. Finally, with a fearful trembling heart she filled the jug at the spring and headed back to the cottage.

Cleotisha arrived home to the loud complaints of her father Draklog, and her three brothers Ishbach, Perzac and Linkot.

"Why is supper so late?' Draklog demanded.

"Yeah, and why were you out gallivanting around when there was work to be done?" Her oldest brother Ishbach put in.

"She was probably daydreaming about being a moon dancer." Linkot, the youngest of the three sneered. Cleotisha barely suppressed her outrage at the verbal abuse that they hurled at her. When they paused in their tirade she briefly explained what had happened. She was shocked by their lack of concern. Didn't they realize that something dreadful had happened? In a loud voice her father commanded Cleotisha to quickly get supper on the table. There would be plenty of time after they had eaten to track down the old bat, Wenoch.

Cleotisha couldn't believe her ears. How could he think of his stomach at a time like this? She certainly had no appetite. She felt as if her stomach was all tied up in knots. Hurriedly she prepared and served the meal to her men folk, and then started the clean up. If they noticed that she didn't eat, none of them mentioned the fact.

After supper, Draklog and his three sons went out. At least they are making a show of looking for grandma, Cleotisha thought. She finished washing the dishes in short order and looked for other jobs to do. She felt that she had to keep busy or she would go crazy. After wiping the counter and table, she swept and mopped the floor, and even scrubbed the stove. Still worrisome thoughts haunted her. Before long, all the work was done and the restlessness overcame her. She paced back and forth like a caged beast. Darkness was descending, so she put fresh seaweed in the brineconc lamps. Normally she found the light from the brineconc seaweed cheerful as it danced and swayed in the liquid that filled the crystal lamps. But tonight it seemed to cast eerie shadows. Oh, what had become of Grandma Wenoch.

The sounds of her father and brothers returning interrupted her brooding thoughts. Draklog looked troubled and shook his massive head in answer to the question in her eyes.

"No luck," he told her. "We thoroughly searched the area surrounding the spring and checked every home in the village. No one has seen her."

Cleotisha ran to her room, threw herself on to her bed, and wept. Would there be no more happy evenings working together on Cleotisha's new dress? How could she ever wear it to dance in the moon festival without her grandma watching proudly from the sidelines? She remembered the pride and happiness that shone in grandma Wenoch's eyes the day they chose Cleotisha to be one of the moon dancers, and now she might never see her again. She cried deep, racking sobs from the depths of her soul. But the aching void, the desperate emptiness, would not go away. Finally, spent and exhausted, she drifted off into a fitful sleep.

Moon Dancers

☽ ● ☾

Chapter two:

SHIMAR SHIFTED HER backpack to a more comfortable position as she trudged up the incline into the mountain pass. She knew the Myrondites lived in the desert on the far side of this coastal range. She was glad that she had brought her winter wrap and a warm blanket with her. The sun had not yet set but there was already a definite chill in the air. She knew that even this early in the fall it could get cold in the mountains at night. She was bone weary from hiking through the foothills all day, with no sleep the night before. She longed for a good place to settle down for the night.

Just then, Shimar noticed a large ginkleberry bush, loaded down with plump juicy fruit. She was as hungry as she was tired. She knew she only had a small supply of food in her pack. Without hesitation, she started picking and eating the delicious berries. To her surprise, as Shimar worked her way around the back of the bush, she discovered a small cave. The low entrance was completely hidden from view behind the ginkleberry bush. She never would have seen it from the path had she not gone around the bush to pick the berries. The cave was too low to stand up in but it would make a good shelter from the cold night winds. That decided, she crawled into the small cave, and made herself a passably comfortable bed out of her warm cloak and her blanket. She was so tired that she fell asleep almost at once.

She was jarred awake sometime later by loud shouts and cracking sounds, and the pounding beat of marching feet. Amongst the noisy confusion, she also heard what sounded like rattling chains and low ghostly moans. "What in the name of the Prenellium City was going on out there?" Shimar felt completely befuddled, largely due to being so rudely awakened out of a sound sleep. Whatever it was sounded like it was right outside her little cave.

Cautiously she peeked out of her hiding place, wondering, in passing, how long she had been asleep. Between the inky blackness of the night that surrounded her, the sleep in her eyes, and the bush in her way, she could see very little. She could only make out the flickering light of many torches approaching along the trail. They were coming from the direction of the Myrondite settlements.

Boldly Shimar crawled out further to where she could peek around the bush and get a better look. She almost gasped aloud when she recognized Lord Salthazar's men in the glow of the torches. What in the name of the Prenellium City were they doing out here? Who were these others with them?

Why were Salthazar's Tephanite soldiers herding these poor people like so many balogs on route to market? Shimar rubbed her eyes and looked again because she couldn't believe what she saw. The people who were being driven so cruelly by the whips of the Tephanite brutes were none other than Myrondites.

One of the towering Tephanite soldiers called a halt right outside Shimar's hiding place. Shimar quickly noted the reason for the delay. One of the Myrondites, a very old man, had collapsed. There was a grumbling of impatience among the Tephanites, while the one who had called the halt poked and prodded the fallen Myrondite with the tip of his spear and kicked at him with his heavy boots.

"Come on! Get up and get moving!" the soldier demanded of the inert mound of rags at his feet. The Myrondite girl, who was chained to the old man, knelt and checked for signs of pulse and breathing.

"He's dead!" she announced quietly.

"Unchain him, roll the body out of the way, and let's get going!" ordered the Tephanite who seemed to be in charge. The soldier stopped prodding at the body, stuck his torch into the sand and bent to obey the command of his superior. He fumbled with the keys momentarily, but soon had the iron shackles off the scrawny ankles of the dead Myrondite. As the burly Tephanite stood up the Myrondite girl made a lunge for the torch and jabbed it in the soldier's face, blinding him. He screamed and clawed at his eyes. As she took off running and stumbling over her chains, she flung the torch into a nearby supply wagon, setting it ablaze. Pandemonium followed.

The Myrondites who were chained to the wagon to pull it, were thrown into a state of panic. Most of the Tephanites were engaged in putting out the fire, and in all the confusion, the rest did not react swiftly enough to catch the fleeing Myrondite girl.

Shimar heard the girl's footsteps, running and stumbling straight towards her. She scrambled to her feet, but before she could retreat to the cave, the Myrondite girl collided with her, and they landed in a tangle of arms and legs behind the ginkleberry bush. Shimar recovered first, and clamped a hand over the girls mouth to stifle a panicked scream. Then, helping the girl onto her hands and knees, she propelled her through the small opening into the cave.

Outside, the Tephanites, having put out the fire, were searching the area for the runaway. The two girls lay in the dark quietness of the cave, hardly daring to breathe. Shimar's heart pounded as heavy footsteps approached their hiding place.

Just when she was sure that they were about to be discovered, the commanding officer gave and order to abandon the search, and continue their march to the forbidden desert. The footsteps retreated. Shimar let out a tortured breath. She was just wondering what to do next when a quiet voice spoke out of the darkness.

"Thank you for helping me. My name is Melki. Who are you? What are you doing way out here?" asked the Myrondite girl.

"I'm Shimar. I'll ask the questions, if you don't mind." Shimar told her coldly. "Where is Jonkin?"

"Who is Jonkin?" Melki asked, puzzled.

"Never mind! It's obvious that you don't know." Shimar grumbled. "Why are Lord Salthazar's men dragging your people off to the slavepits?"

"Because we refuse to call him Lord or pay him tribute." came the terse reply.

Shimar was taken aback. In spite of all the horrible stories she had heard about the Myrondites, she had to admire their spunk. This girl, Melki certainly had plenty. The girls remained quiet for a time, each lost in their own thoughts. Presently the silence was broken by the sound of rock clanging against metal.

"What in the name of the Prenellium City are you doing?" Shimar demanded in an irritated voice.

"I'm trying to get these shackles off. They hurt." Melki replied in a quiet voice that trembled slightly.

"Here, let me see what I can do." offered Shimar.

After fumbling and feeling around in her pack for a moment or two, she was able to locate both the torch and the flint to light it. Presently the small cave was filled with a warm glow, and Shimar got her first good look at the Myrondite girl. Melki appeared to be about the same age as Shimar, though much smaller in stature. Soft brown eyes peered back at Shimar from beneath thick black bangs. The rest of Melki's hair was pulled back snuggly into one long braid down her back, exposing a pair of rather large pointed ears. Her skin was a deep copper brown, and her clothing simple and plain. Then Shimar cringed inwardly as her gaze fell on the swollen, bleeding ankles encased in the heavy metal shackles. There was just enough chain connecting them to allow the girl to walk.

"We have got to get these off!" Shimar declared vehemently. "I wonder if I can pick the lock."

After handing the torch to the Myrondite girl, and another rummage in her pack, Shimar produced a few small tools. Working on the locks took persistence, but eventually she was successful. Shimar took back the torch and handed Melki the blanket.

"Here. Try to get some sleep. Tomorrow we shall see what can be done for your poor ankles."

"Thank you." Melki murmured softly.

With that, Shimar extinguished the light and curled up in her cloak. Soon both girls were fast asleep.

Fifteen-year old Jerah stretched, and pushed her tousled blonde curls out of her sleepy blue eyes. Throwing back the covers, and climbing out of bed, she crossed the room to look out the window. The bright sunshine that they had enjoyed the day before had been replaced by a dense purple fog that hid the sea from view.

The men would be staying home. No one was foolish enough to go out fishing when the purple fog rolled in. Judging by the sound of the waves crashing on the shore, it was probably just as well. It would be very rough out on the water today. Jerah didn't really mind it when it was stormy. Indeed, she loved the Zicktel Sea in all its varying moods.

After dressing quickly, and pulling a brush through her thick golden curls, Jerah strolled out into the main room of the cottage. There she found her father in his favorite chair by the fire, reading a book. The door to her brothers' room was closed. With the boat not going out today, it didn't surprise Jerah that Kendrig and Bretlig would choose to sleep in. Jerah's mother was an early riser, so it seemed odd that she was not up, bustling about fixing breakfast.

"Good morning princess. How is the prettiest moon dancer this morning?" her father greeted her cheerfully.

"I'm just fine. Where is mother?" Jerah asked.

"She was still in bed when I came out here, but I would have thought she would be up by now." her father replied as he set aside his book and rose from his chair.

"It isn't like her to sleep in." Jerah stated emphatically. "You don't suppose she is sick or something, do you?" Without waiting for a reply, she marched purposefully to the door of her parents' bedroom and knocked. When this brought no response from within, she pushed open the door. Her father was right behind her as they peered into the room. The window was closed and the bed unmade. There was no sign of Jerah's mother.

"Where could she be? What are we to do? Oh what has become of her?" Jerah's voice rose in panic. Her father's face was ashen. For a moment he could not speak. When he did find his voice, it came out in a violent eruption.

"No! Not Lithriss! Not her too!" He shook his head sadly. His voice trembled, and his blue eyes were full of fear. "I don't know what to make of these disappearances, but it is past time to act. The elders must do something!"

Normally fourteen-year-old Resha loved looking after her adorable baby brother Cheran, but today there was something else she wanted to do. She stroked the silky rose-colored material lovingly as she held it up to herself, surveying the result in the full-length mirror. Solemn brown eyes peered back at her from under a mane of chestnut curls. The color of the material matched the pink of her cheeks. She had chosen well. She could picture what her dress would look like when it was completed. She could see herself wearing it as she dipped and twirled with the other dancers at the festival. It would be a night like no other, filled with music, stardust and enchantment.

She could hardly wait to get started on her sewing, but that as well as her daydreaming would have to wait for the time being. With a sigh, she reluctantly lay down the delicate, beautiful cloth, and went to take charge of her baby brother, Cheran, so that her parents could attend the meeting called by the elders. "I sure hope they find out what happened to the missing people." Resha thought with a worried frown on her face.

Cheran sat on the furs in front of the galgabite fireplace, making cooing sounds and contentedly playing with his toes. Resha had to admit he was a good baby, not fussy like some. When he saw Resha, he gave a squeal of delight and lifted his arms to be picked up. He had already had his lunch, and soon it would be time for his afternoon nap. Once Cheran fell asleep, she didn't think her parents would mind if she worked on her dress until he woke up.

Resha stood up and stretched with a yawn. The dress was coming along nicely, although there was still a fair piece of work left to do. A glance at the clock informed her that it was later than she had supposed.

"Cheran must be awake by now." she said to herself, "I wonder why I haven't heard him."

Quietly she opened the door to the bedroom, and was met by an icy blast of sea air. Resha knew she had fastened the window securely from the inside when she put Cheran down for his nap. Now it was wide open. Surely, the baby couldn't manage to unfasten and open the window, even if he could somehow get out of his crib and reach it. At that moment, she noticed to her horror that the crib was empty. Terror gripped her heart as she realized that, although she could not fathom how, someone must have crept in through the window and stolen the baby away while she had been happily sewing in the next room.

Judging from the frosty coolness of the room the window had been open for more than just a few minutes. Falling to her knees she checked under her parent's bed to make sure Cheran had not crawled there. Her search revealed nothing but a few dust bunnies. She rose to her feet. There was nowhere else for the baby to hide. Oh what should she do? Resha grabbed her cloak and a brineconc lamp and hurried to check the area underneath the window for footprints or some other clue.

The purple fog not only impaired her vision, but made familiar objects appear ghostly and unreal. Resha's home looked sinister and brooding. Even her favorite gumphalus tree loomed large and menacing in front of her. As she hurried around to the back of the house, she almost collided with her best friend Nordelia, and Nordelia's tall slim brother Abiud.

"By the moons! What's going on here?" Abiud asked.

"Cheran is missing! It's all my fault!" wailed Resha hysterically.

"Great Balogs!" was all Abiud could think to say.

"Are you sure he's gone? Tell us what happened." Nordelia's pretty, violet eyes were full of concern. Slowly, between great gulping sobs, Resha told them the story. After trying to reassure her, Abiud and Nordelia joined Resha in examining the area underneath the bedroom window. The ground in that spot was gravel so it was not too surprising when they found no footprints. Search as they might, they were unable to uncover any other clue either.

"It's like he vanished into thin air." Abiud shook his head in disbelief.

"I wish I knew what we could do to help." Nordelia said sympathetically.

"How can I tell my parents? And what about grandpa Mibzar? How am I going to face them? This is like a nightmare. It doesn't seem real somehow, but my darling baby brother is really and truly gone!" With this Resha slumped to the ground and wept uncontrollably. Nordelia sat down beside her and took her hand. Abiud, not knowing what else to do, gave Resha a couple of reassuring pats on the shoulder.

Moon Dancers

☽ ● ☾

Chapter three:

JERAH PACED IMPATIENTLY across the main room of the cottage, her mind clouded with troubled thoughts. Would her mother and the others who were missing, ever be found? What had the council of elders decided to do? Would they go ahead with the moon festival as planned? If so, who would take Shimar's place? Were the Myrondites responsible for the disappearances? Would her people go to war against the Myrondites? Her mind buzzed with a hundred questions.

She could hear the waves crashing wildly on the shore. Jerah longed to do something. She found it so hard to just sit and wait. She felt as restless as the sea sounded.

The darkness outside was not due just to the fog and the storm. The hour was growing late. The meeting should be over by now. Why had her father and Kendrig not returned? Jerah sighed as she filled the crystal lamps with fresh brineconc seaweed. As a child, she had always watched the brineconc lamps with fascination, but tonight filling the lamps was just another job to do. Jerah found that it did little to distract her from her worrisome thoughts.

"It's not fair!" declared Bretlig, Jerah's stalky, twelve-year old brother, as he stormed into the room. "Kendrig gets to do everything because he's the oldest. I wanted to go to the meeting, too. How are we supposed to find out anything when we're stuck at home like this?"

"I know." Jerah acknowledged sympathetically, "but at the moment there isn't a whole lot we can do about it."

"Even if we do go to war against the Myrondites, I probably won't get to fight. Father would say I'm too young." Bretlig grumbled with a defiant toss of his head of blonde curls.

"Yes, I'm quite sure father feels that you are not yet old enough to go into battle." Jerah tried to hide an amused smile.

"It's not fair! I always miss out on all the action!" Bretlig stomped his foot in frustration.

"Come and sit down. Perhaps if we put our heads together we can come up with a plan." Jerah invited as she plopped down on the rug infront of the galgabite fireplace, and patted the spot beside her.

"Yeah? What kind of plan?" he asked as he sprawled out next to her.

Jerah didn't answer immediately. Instead, she sat up and poked absently at the fire, then added a couple of pieces of wood. As the sticks burst into flames, she quietly said, "Well, I guess the first thing we need to do is find out what went on at the meeting. That is, once the meeting is over."

"Oh the meeting has been over for a while now. Father and Kendrig went down to the docks with a number of the other men to secure the boats that were threatening to break loose from their mooring in the storm." Bretlig informed her.

"And just how do you know all this?" inquired Jerah "On second thought, never mind. I don't want to know. Since you seem to have ways of acquiring information, how do you suggest that we find out about the meeting?"

"We have to ask someone who was there, but whom? Father never tells us anything! Besides, I don't want to wait around until he gets back." pondered Bretlig, as he rose to his feet and paced impatiently.

"Okay, so who was at the meeting that will talk to us?" asked Jerah "It has to be someone who would not have gone down to the dock to help with the boats."

"Why don't we ask old Greplog?" Bretlig suggested.

"Do we dare? After all, he is one of the elders......" Jerah paused, and then suddenly declared "Let's do it! Of course, it will have to be done delicately. We don't want him to suspect that he is being pumped for information."

"Come on then! Let's go!" Bretlig called over his shoulder as he headed out the door. Jerah had to chuckle. Delicately was not Bretlig's method of doing anything.

Jerah was lost in thought as she got up and followed at a more sedate pace. It did not take long to traverse the short distance to the home of their friend Greplog. Yes, Greplog was a friend, and very wise, though he did act odd at times. Some said he was becoming senile due to his advanced years, but Greplog had always been the same lovable but queer old fellow as long as Jerah could remember. She wondered what they would find him doing. Would he be staring out at the night sky with his powerful lens? Would he be pouring over his numerous books and charts, seeking out some obscure piece of information of interest only to him? Or perhaps he would be scribbling on bits of paper, working out calculations, equations and formulas that only he could understand.

When they quietly entered Greplog's small home, which was in its usual state of disarray, he was involved in none of the aforementioned activities. Instead, he was pacing the floor, muttering to himself, while his boney fingers stroked his long grey beard.

"So are we going to war against the Myrondites or not?" Bretlig blurted out before Jerah could stop him, or announce their presence in a more civilized manner. Greplog whirled around to face them with a startled look on his face. Upon recognizing them, his expression dissolved into one of amusement.

"Why, no Lad. Not at present anyway." Greplog said good-naturedly.

"I am sorry we startled you but…" Jerah apologized for Bretlig, who apparently did not think to do so. "Oh, Greplog, they have taken mom… Others are missing too. Oh, what does it all mean?" Her shoulders shook as tears rolled down her cheeks. Bretlig rolled his eyes as he looked at Greplog.

"Girls! It is just that we are worried about the disappearances and the rumors about Myrondites…"

"And you have come to grill me about the meeting." Greplog said in a solemn tone that was contradicted by the twinkle in his eyes.

"So are you going to tell us the news or not?" Bretlig asked cheekily.

"There is not a lot to tell. It was decided that there was not enough evidence to link the disappearances to the Myrondites. So, for now there will be no war." Greplog informed them in a voice that was genuinely serious this time.

"What about the Moon Festival?" Jerah asked hesitantly.

"It has been decided to go ahead with the festival as planned." Greplog replied.

Jerah couldn't believe her ears. How could they expect Jerah and the other girls to dance the moon dance with joyful abandon, the way it was meant to be danced, while they were mourning loved ones who were missing.

"But what about Shimar?" Jerah wondered aloud.

"She will be replaced by Nordelia. It seems that she has been practicing with her friend Resha, and should do just fine" Greplog told them. "At least none of the other dancers are missing......yet." The last word was spoken softly, barely above a whisper, but it seemed to echo ominously in the silence that followed Greplog's words. Jerah shuddered as a sudden chill ran down her back. Bretlig had become strangely quiet.

Nordelia ran her fastest through the yellow, wide-spreading gumphalas trees. Her heart pounded in her chest as she pushed herself harder, ignoring the stitch in her side. She must reach the others at once! Lives might depend on it. Her lungs screamed protests against exploding pain. She battled on until she broke into the clearing where all the Crolarmites were gathered to prepare for the moon festival. Collapsing breathlessly in front of those near by, she managed to gasp out

"They're gone! All four of the others have disappeared."

"Whatever do you mean?" Resha's grandfather, Mibzar asked, unable to believe what he was hearing.

"The other dancers!" She blurted out "They're gone!"

"It can't be!" Mibzar exclaimed in shocked disbelief. After all, his own granddaughter was among the four. His precious baby grandson was already among those who had gone missing, so for anything to have befallen Resha was unthinkable.

"Oh how I wish it were not so!" Nordelia moaned, her slender body trembled and her shoulders were slumped in despair. "But they have really and truly vanished. We were practicing the dance. I only left them for a few moments to fetch some water and when I got back they were gone!"

The other Crolarmites within hearing distance had been shocked momentarily into a stunned silence, but now that the news had begun to sink in, they started murmuring among themselves. Draklog threw his fur-trimmed mantel from his massive shoulders and leapt upon a large rock, stomping his heavy boot clad feet. His unruly mane of red hair, combined with the look of fury on his face made him quite a formidable sight. He gestured wildly with his large ham fists as his voice boomed out over the crowd.

"This is the dirty work of the Myrondites!" he raged. "What about all the other people who are missing? You know how the Myrondites crave slaves and now they have broken the festival truce with this heinous act! I say we march at once! Fellow Crolarmites to arms! This is war!"

"Not so my brothers!" Mibzar called out over the crowd. His regal appearance commanded attention. His long white beard swayed from side to side as he shook his head sadly. "It is true that the Myrondites are our ancient enemies but we have no proof that they are the ones responsible for these disappearances. Let us not jump to hasty conclusions that we are likely to regret later."

"Mibzar is right!" Greplog agreed firmly. "The more I study this, the more convinced I become that it is not the Myrondites who are to blame. No, this smells of evil magic."

"I agree with Greplog!" Kendrig spoke up "I too believe there is evil magic at work here. The Myrondites do not have magic anymore than we do. So who is the only powerful sorcerer that we know of?"

"Do you realize what you are saying?" Mibzar sputtered, "It couldn't have been him!"

"And why not?" Kendrig demanded. His square chin thrust out defiantly, and his blue eyes sparked a challenge. Both his mother and sister were among those missing, so he was determined to have his say. He tossed his head of short blonde curls and stared boldly at those around, daring them to disagree. "You pay tribute to him because you are afraid of him. You fear to even mention his name, but I shall. Yes, I believe that it is Lord Salthazar himself who is at the bottom of all this. We must look for the dancers and the others who are missing in the slave pits in the forbidden desert." Mibzar was speechless. His face turned as white as his beard, but Greplog smiled at Kendrig approvingly.

"But could even Lord Salthazar have accomplished all this without inside help?" Abuid asked. His long fingers nervously brushed back his brown bangs from his long forehead. His large hazel eyes were solemn and frightened.

"This is all nonsense!" Draklog scoffed, dismissing what Kendrig had said with a motion of his hand. "Lord Salthazar offers us his protection. He has never turned against us before. Why should he suddenly choose to do so now?"

"But what if Kendrig is right? Even without his magic, we would not stand a chance against his huge army of Tephanite soldiers. We are doomed!" Nordelia wailed.

Eliphaz's gray eyes darted furtively around. The forest glade was already full of shadows as twilight approached. A frown appeared on his pointed weasel-like face. He pulled his cloak closer about his small frame and shuffled his feet impatiently.

It was imperative that he get a message to Draklog at once. Would that boy never get here? At that moment, a rustling in the bushes announced the arrival of Draklog's son, Ishbach.

"So, what is so important that it couldn't wait until tomorrow?" Ishbach spoke flippantly. He gave an arrogant toss of his head, his thick mane of hair shone red like copper in the setting sun.

"Don't you think I would have waited had it been something trivial?" Eliphaz said in a condescending tone. The young man's piercing green eyes narrowed.

"Well what is it then?" Ishbach said with annoyance.

"You are to give this message to your father Draklog. Make sure that no one else sees it." Eliphaz ordered. "Do you understand?" Here he handed Ishbach a folded piece of paper. Ishbach started to unfold the paper in order to read the message. "Not here you fool!" Eliphaz exploded, peering suspiciously at the bushes and trees that surrounded them, as if fearing that they were being watched.

"What ever you say." Ishbach said with a shrug of his broad shoulders as he refolded the paper and tucked it inside his cloak. With that he turned and casually strolled back the way he had come. Eliphaz stood watching after him for a moment before he melted into the shadows.

Moon Dancers

☽ ● ☾

Chapter four:

IN SPITE OF the clutter that was strewn about, the dimly lit room had a cozy atmosphere. Bookshelves lined the walls, and comfortable chairs snuggled around an ornate rug in front of a galgabite fireplace. The cheerfully crackling fire was in sharp contrast to the serious expressions on the faces of the four young people gathered at the home of the elder that night.

"Tell us why you are convinced that it is Lord Salthazar who is doing all this?" Abiud asked quietly.

"Oh I have my ways." Greplog nodded knowingly.

"He learns much from all the ancient books he reads," Bretlig piped up before Greplog had a chance to reply further, "but mostly he just knows things. After a while you learn not to question how."

"And have you learned that lesson well enough to teach it to another, my inquisitive lad?" asked the elder. He turned to Abiud, winked, and added, "I tell you, the questions he has asked me would fill more books than even I would care to read." Bretlig's face turned red. He opened his mouth as if to speak, then thought better of it.

"I only have one question. What is to be done?" Kendrig spoke up. "Must we sit back and do nothing while someone as evil as Lord Salthazar takes over the whole land, spiriting away whoever he chooses to his slave pits in the forbidden desert?"

"I know you have all been through a lot. I fear you will suffer much more before we are through." Greplog shook his head sadly.

"But is there no way to defeat Lord Salthazar?" Bretlig cried out in desperation.

"The only one who has the power to defeat Lord Salthazar is the High King." the old Crolarmite told them.

"Then we must seek him." Nordelia said simply.

"That may be easier said than done." warned the elder.

"But does not the King desire us to seek him?" Abiud was puzzled.

"Indeed he does, and it is to him you must go for help, but I fear that you will find many obstacles in your path." Greplog replied. He took a sip from his cup of herbal tea, then shifted some papers on the small table beside him to make room to set down his mug.

"Do you mean that Lord Salthazar will try to stop us?" Kendrig asked.

"That is one part of it. As soon as he finds out that you are seeking the King he is sure to do all in his power to prevent you from reaching him," Greplog explained, "but I think you may find yourselves to be the biggest obstacle of all. You see our people turned their back on the High King many generations ago. They chose to follow Lord Salthazar and pay him tribute instead. So we are not on the best terms with the King."

"Is it true that the King lives in the Prenellium City up in the high northern mountains?" inquired Bretlig, as he sprawled on the rug by their feet. "The ancient books say it is so." Greplog declared. That obviously settled the matter as far as he was concerned. He lovingly fingered an old volume on the shelf beside him. "There is an ancient prophesy that the King's only son, the Prince himself, will defeat Lord Salthazar."

"I have heard a little about the High King and the Prenellium City, but I have never heard of an heir to the throne. Tell us more about this Prince." Kendrig sat forward in his chair as if ready for action.

"It is not surprising that you don't know about him! Few Crolarmites these days know anything about the King, let alone his son. I don't know any who give them the respect and honor that they are due." Greplog replied with a sad shake of his grey head.

"It's all there for anyone who cares to take the time to study. The ancient manuscripts are full of stories of how the Prince will someday come and free us from Lord Salthazar's grasp. Then he will set up his kingdom of peace and plenty that will never end."

"I didn't know that the ancient books talked about Lord Salthazar!" Nordelia was astonished at the discovery.

"Oh, they mention him, although not by name. As powerful as that evil tyrant is, his power is nothing compared to that of the High King." Greplog slapped his palm with his fist to emphasize his point.

"Why hasn't he already dealt with Salthazar? What is he waiting for?" Bretlig wanted to know. His fingers nervously played with a frayed edge of the carpet.

"The King's timing is not our timing. He will act when the time is right."

Greplog assured them. "I believe it will be soon."

"So, are we to journey to the Prenellium City up in the northern mountains? That is such a long way! Won't it be dangerous?" Nordelia asked nervously.

"Yes Indeed. It will be very dangerous. Unfortunately, I fear that it is no longer safe here, either." the old Crolarmite replied.

"I say we should sneak into Salthazar's fortress in the forbidden desert." Bretlig grumbled. "Isn't that where the missing people are supposed to be? I say we go to the slave pits."

"Go to the slave pits and do what my lad?" Greplog gently reprimanded him. "Just how would it help your mother and sister, and all the others who are missing, for you to become one of Salthazar's many slaves? Do not fool yourself into thinking you could get into the fortress undetected. Salthazar would know you were coming while you were still miles away."

"Even though I am a bit nervous about the journey to the Prenellium City, I am more afraid of Lord Salthazar and the slave pits, than I am of the High King." Nordelia spoke shyly.

"So we must make preparations to go to the High King." Kendrig said with a note of finality. He stood up and stretched.

"Yes! And quickly!" The elder was adamant. "I have a feeling that there is not much time left. You should leave at once!"

A heavy darkness filled the throne room and hung thick in the stale air. This was only partly due to the fact that Lord Salthazar's throne room was deep inside his galgabite fortress; a structure whose windows were few and small.

The dark gray stonewalls were cold and clammy and gave off a musty odor. The two smoky torches mounted on the wall did little to dispel the oppressive blackness of the immense room. They only succeeded in casting eerie shadows, adding to the gloom of the place.

The tall figure on the throne was imposing indeed. He was dressed in a long black cloak that was fastened at his throat with a large ruby broach.

His thin pale face seemed illuminated in sharp contrast to the darkness that permeated the room. Anger and hate burned in his red eyes, and his thin claw-like hands were clenched into fists. The fury on his face was enough to strike fear into even the bravest heart. Before him stood a high ranking Tephanite officer, quaking in his boots.

"You incompetent fool! I gave you a simple task. You were to bring me the five moon dancers." Salthazar hissed, barely above a whisper, "As well as some one near and dear to each of them, in order to insure the dancers' cooperation. Why is it that we only have four moon dancers? How is it that you and your men let one of them escape?" Although he spoke softly, his words echoed ominously in the massive throne room.

Yorg-Dogmah could not find his voice. "Oh No! I am really in for it this time." the hulking brute thought. "It's bad enough when he yells, but he is really dangerous when he whispers!"

"You and your men will march at once!" the black cloaked figure on the throne commanded. "Attack the village! Bring them all back as slaves! Kill any who resist! Bring me that girl! If you fail, again I shall be most displeased. You don't want that, do you?" Here Salthazar leaned forward as if ready to pounce. He stared intently at the quivering mountain of muscle before him, demanding an answer.

"Of course not my Lord." Yorg-Dogmah stammered, not daring to look into those piercing red eyes. "I assure you that there will be no mistake this time. We will have the girl here before the moons are full."

"See that you do." was the only reply, but it carried a threat that hung tangibly in the air.

Draklog scanned the paper that he held in his large hands. He had read it over so many times that he could probably recite it from memory. Why did Eliphaz have to dump this responsibility onto his shoulders? In angry frustration, Draklog crumpled the paper up and tossed it into the flames that crackled in the galgabite fireplace in front of him.

He was well aware that this action changed nothing. Still it gave him a small measure of satisfaction to watch the paper consumed by the blaze. Draklog sat there in his overstuffed arm chair, staring into the flames, as if he hoped to find the answer there. He had the uncomfortable feeling that perhaps they were going a little too far this time, but he could see no way of getting around it.

Just then, his three sons traipsed into the room. Ishbac, the oldest, flopped into the only other comfortable chair in the room. His two brothers sprawled on the fur rug by Draklog's feet.

"So, are we going to carry out the wild plan that Eliphaz came up with?" Ishbac wanted to know.

"I don't see that we have much choice." Draklog grumbled into his beard.

"But can we pull it off? Can we really make it seem as if the Myrondites are attacking the village?" Perzac, the youngest inquired. He sat and propped his head up with his elbow. Clear blue eyes peered intently at his father from under an unruly mass of red curls.

"We have to make it work." Draklog pronounced darkly. His green eyes looked troubled as they gazed back at the freckled face of his youngest son. "I just hope Eliphaz knows what he's getting us into."

Nordelia's heart pounded as she scurried down the forest path in the deepening twilight. Her lovely violet eyes, wide with fear looked much too large for her small pale face. Her long, sandy blonde hair streamed out behind as she rushed past the old gnarled stumps and trees of the forest as fast as her short legs could carry her. Who knew what horrors lay hidden behind those trees; watching; waiting........ A sudden breeze brought the trees to life, transforming them into grotesque monsters, greedily reaching out spidery claws to grab her.

It was more than the chilly night air that caused Nordelia to shudder. It was easy to let her imagination run wild in these woods at night. Especially when she knew that, they were fleeing from very real danger. A twig snapped. Nordelia jumped. Then she realized that she was the one who had stepped on it. Even so, she could not resist the urge to glance over her shoulder to see if they were being pursued.

Would they really be able to escape with their lives? Or would they be hunted down and destroyed by the Tephanite soldiers who had attacked and ransacked their village? Was there even one place of safety left in all the land of Ku-Lammorah? Greplog thought so, and he was convinced that only the High King could help them. Most of the Crolarmites of her village thought that the ancient writings were merely myths and legends, and thought Greplog was crazy for believing them to be true. Now those who had not been slaughtered outright by the Tephanite soldiers had been hauled off to the slave pits. Only Kendrig, Bretlig, Abuid and Nordelia, the four young people warned by Greplog, had managed to escape.

As Nordelia hurried to catch up with the others, her forehead wrinkled into a worried frown. They rushed on down the trail while the woods grew steadily darker and more shadowy. Soon even the strange half-light of dusk was gone. The deep darkness of the forest night surrounded them. They were about to stop and rest until morning, when they spotted the flicker of a campfire through the trees up ahead.

"Kendrig!" Nordelia whispered urgently. "Someone is there."

"Yes, I wonder who it could be." Kendrig spoke softly. "I think we had better find out."

"Do we have to?" Nordelia was sure she would rather not know.

"Of course we do! don't be such a baby!" retorted Bretlig.

"Shush! Keep your voice down." warned Kendrig. "Now follow me as quietly as you can. If possible we want to find out who it is without them knowing we are here."

Nordelia's heart was filled with dread as they inched slowly towards the glow of the flames. She felt sure that whoever was by the fire must have been alerted to their presence by the occasionally snapping twig or rustling bush caused by their passage. After what seemed like an eternity, they had crept up to where they could peek through the bushes into the small clearing. Nordelia's worst fears were confirmed. There was no mistaking the ten brutes around the fire for anything but Tephanite soldiers.

Their tall thick bodies sprawled lazily on the ground. Their huge gnarled hands held pieces of meat that they had cooked over the open flames. They greedily devoured their meal, ripping off large chunks with their big sharp teeth. The reflection of the flickering firelight danced menacingly in their round yellow eyes. Their pale gray skin had a deathly pallor, which the firelight did little to enhance. One of the hulking brutes ran his big greasy fingers through his wild bushy hair, and then scratched behind one of his large pointed ears. Nordelia cringed when she noticed a pile of rather wicked looking weapons stacked nearby.

Abiud was staring with his eyes and mouth wide open, completely engrossed in the scene before them. Suddenly the breeze changed direction, sending smoke from the fire towards him in great smothering billows. He got a big choking mouthful and could not help but cough.

"What was that?" One of the horrible creatures growled. They all rose swiftly to their feet and headed straight for the small group of frightened Crolarmites.

"Run!" Kendrig gave the unnecessary command, as the four young people fled back down the path in the direction from, which they had come. With her shorter legs, Nordelia soon fell behind the others. The long legged brutes were gaining fast. Nordelia could hear them crashing through the bushes right behind her, and could not resist a glance over her shoulder to see just how close they were. At that moment her foot caught in a root and she tripped, falling flat on her face. Before she could regain her feet the Tephanites had surrounded her. She was so frightened that when she tried to scream, no sound would come out. A rag was stuffed into her mouth and another was tied tightly over top. Her hands and feet were bound with coarse rope, and then one of the horrible creatures effortlessly threw her over his shoulder and carried her back to the campfire. After they had unceremoniously plunked her down, the brutes went back to their meal as if nothing had happened.

Nordelia's Captors had placed her closer to the fire than was comfortable. The side of her nearest the flame was painfully hot, and occasional sparks shot out and landed on her. Smoke billowed in her face, stinging her eyes and choking her. With the dirty gag in her mouth, she felt like she couldn't breath. Her arms and legs were beginning to grow numb because the ropes had been tied so tightly that they bit cruelly into her flesh and hampered her circulation. Desperately she tried to loosen her bonds, but the harder she tried the more they dug in. She could see no possible means of escape. All looked hopeless. Hot tears welled up in her eyes and spilled down her cheeks in big drops.

Moon Dancers

☽ ● ☾

Chapter five:

Nordelia was not sure how much time had past, but the Tephanites had long since finished their meal, and the fire was dying down, when a rustling sound alerted them. At a signal from the Gunja, the ranking officer of the small group, two of the soldiers went to investigate. They returned in less than a minute, pushing Kendrig, Bretlig and Abiud in front of them. Nordelia's heart sank. They had come back in an attempt to rescue her. Now they were all in the hands of the terrible Tephanites.

"Look what we found!" one of the brutes declared proudly.

"Tie them up!" the Gunja commanded. The three young Crolarmites were bound hand and foot with coarse ropes, and thrown to the ground beside Nordelia. The Gunja approached with a cruel sneer on his ugly face. "Where is the other moon dancer? If you know what is good for you, you will tell me quickly where to find her." he demanded.

"You don't suppose that she could be the one that we are looking for, do you?" ventured one of the brutes, indicating Nordelia with a jab of his finger. "Don't be an idiot! The girl we are looking for is tall with dark hair, this one is small with fair hair." the Gunja scoffed. Turning on Kendrig, he ordered, "Tell me where Shimar is!"

"I don't know where Shimar is." Kendrig answered truthfully. "I had assumed that she was with the others in the slave pits."

"Enough lies!" the brute raged in fury. "Talk now, or suffer the consequences!"

"But I told you the truth...." Kendrig began. Whatever else he might have said at that point, was cut off by the stinging blow of the Gunja's hand across his face. Nordelia winced as she saw the bright red mark left on Kendrig's cheek, and the small trickle of blood at the corner of his mouth.

"Fetch me the irons!" the Gunja barked. One of the Tephanites scurried to obey.

Kendrig grew silent. He had nothing to tell them, and he knew it would do no good to argue with these barbarians. To her horror, Nordelia saw that the iron rods that the Tephanite brought were red hot from the fire. The Gunja took one in each hand, grasping them firmly by their wooden handles, and headed menacingly towards Kendrig. He held the ends of the hot irons dangerously close to Kendrig's eyes. Nordelia was afraid to watch, but somehow she could not bring herself to look away.

"Why don't you ask her?" one of the brutes suggested, indicating Nordelia with a tip of his shaggy head. The Gunja stopped in his tracks and turned towards Nordelia with a wicked grin on his ugly face.

"Yes! I am sure that she can be persuaded to give us the information that we seek."

"Leave her alone!" Kendrig demanded bravely.

"So, you don't wish any harm to come to the girl!" the Tephanite crowed triumphantly. "Then you had better start talking or she will learn the meaning of the word pain."

"All right! You win! I'll talk!" Kendrig called out. "Shimar is not far from here. She is only about two miles east of here, where the two creeks flow together into one. She is hiding there in a hollow stump."

"That's better. Now to teach you not to defy me in the future....." the Gunja touched the hot irons on Kendrig's cheek. There was a hissing sound and the smell of scorched flesh. Kendrig cried out in pain and pulled back. "You had better be telling the truth." the Tephanite warned as he tossed the irons back into the fire.

Nordelia winced at the horrible burn on Kendrig's face. It would be a nasty scar. She just hoped Kendrig knew what he was doing, making up that story. Despite his threats, she could tell the Tephanite brute believed the lies, but she could not help worrying. As the Gunja dispatched four men to go and fetch Shimar, Nordelia found herself wondering what he would do when they did not find her. Where was Shimar? What did the Tephanites want with the moon dancers anyway? What would they do if they knew that she had been named as Shimar's replacement? Nordelia did not want to think about it, but her mind kept going around in circles.

The Gunja posted a guard, then he and the remaining Tephanites lay down and were soon fast asleep. This was the opportunity that Kendrig was waiting for. His eye was on the guard. Whenever the Tephanite's attention was diverted from them for a few seconds, Kendrig inched backward towards the dying embers of the campfire. He froze whenever the guard looked their way, hoping that he would not notice the slight change of position. Once he was close enough to the remains of the campfire, Kendrig slowly and deliberately placed the ropes that bound his hands against the glowing coals. It was too hot to have his hands so close to the embers for long, and the task was made more difficult by the fact that his hands were tied behind his back so he could not see what he was doing. Besides, he had to keep his eye on the guard to make sure that he did not notice what was going on beneath his nose.

Because he could not see, he burned his hands on the coals, making it even more difficult to force himself to keep them so near the heat. It was hard enough not to cry out, but Kendrig was sure that his face must reveal the pain he was enduring. A glance at the tears that shimmered in Nordelia's lovely violet eyes confirmed that she knew what he was trying to do and what it was costing him.

Finally, Kendrig's persistence paid off. The ropes that bound his hands burned through. His hands began to ache from holding them behind his back as if they were still tied up. He was feeling impatient, but he knew he must wait for just the right moment. If he made his move too soon their attempted escape would be discovered and swiftly thwarted. If he waited too long the other four Tephanites might return, and then all would be lost.

At last, the guard's head drooped forward and his snores could be heard above those of the other Tephanites. Kendrig hastily untied his legs. As stealthily as possible, he took a dagger from the stack of Tephanite weapons and freed the others. Somehow, in spite of legs that felt like limp noodles from being tied up, they managed to tiptoe from the Tephanite camp. They were almost free and clear when one of the sleeping brutes stirred, groaned, and rolled over. The four escapees froze like statues, hardly daring to breathe. Fortunately the ugly fellow went back to sleep without even opening his eyes.

Once they were far enough from the camp that they were unlikely to wake the Tephanites, Kendrig gave the signal and they broke into a run. The plan now was to put as much distance between themselves and the sleeping brutes as possible.

Before long, the first gray streaks of dawn appeared on the eastern horizon. As night gave way to the new day, everything took on an enchanted silver hue. Drops of dew glistened on the branches like diamonds. The air smelled fresh and clean. The birds filled the morning with music. The whole forest seemed to be coming alive to celebrate the freedom of the four travelers. The sunrise turned the clouds into fluffy pink feathers and the peachy glow crowned the eastern mountains.

Shimar and the Myrondite girl, Melki were relaxing by a little mountain brook. The morning sunshine filtered through the canopy of large yellow leaves overhead. Shimar leaned against the sturdy trunk of a gumphalas tree. One of her long legs was stretched out, the other knee was up with her arms wrapped around it.

Melki sat on the grassy bank with her feet dangling in the cool water. The swelling had gone down, and her ankles looked much better.

"You've had a couple of days to rest up. I am sure you are ready to travel now. Your reluctance has nothing to do with your ankles. You are nervous about the idea of going back with me to my village, aren't you? You have probably heard many exaggerated stories about my people, just as I have about yours. Myrondites don't really drink blood, do they?" Shimar asked.

"We most certainly do not." Melki assured her. "We do sacrifice a young daulph on the harvest full moons. The same time you have that moon festival of yours. The animals' blood is shed as a sin offering, and then the meat is cooked as the main dish at the feast. We all drink a small glass of red ginkleberry wine with the supper. It is a symbol of the innocent blood shed to atone for our sins."

"So what horror stories have you been told about us?" Shimar inquired.

"That your men are giant, foul tempered ogres with fiery red hair, almost as bad as the Tephanites." Melki told her.

"Well, there is one man in my village that comes close to that description." Shimar admitted with a chuckle, as she thought of Draklog. "If we rest today, do you think you will be up to traveling tomorrow?" she asked the Myrondite girl. "It's only a few days till the full moons, and I had hoped to be home by then. I just wish I knew what had happened to Jonkin." she finished with a wistful sigh.

"Do you really think it's a good idea for me to come back to your village with you?" Melki was hesitant.

"Well I certainly can't leave you here by yourself. Where else would you go? From what I understand there isn't anything left of your village but a few burned out ruins." Shimar blurted out impatiently. Melki grew strangely silent. She wiped at her eyes with the back of her hand, but her cheeks were damp and her lips quivered.

"Look, I'm sorry. That was thoughtless of me." Shimar spoke quietly as she moved closer and placed a hand on the other girl's trembling shoulder. Melki was slumped over with her face buried in her hands.

"Just leave me alone." came the muffled reply.

Suddenly, Melki sat bolt upright, her eyes wide with fear. They had both heard it. There was no mistaking the heavy marching feet or the sound of cracking whips. The Tephanite soldiers must have attacked another Myrondite village, and now they were approaching along the path. Any minute now, the evil parade would pass by just above where the girls were sitting down by the creek bed. Hurriedly they dove for cover in some nearby underbrush.

Branches poked at Shimar and Melki as they crouched in the bushes, holding their breath, waiting for the Tephanites and their luckless captives to go past. To the dismay of the two girls however, the procession called a halt right above them. They heard someone shout orders for the water barrels to be filled, then two of the soldiers came scrambling down the same bank that Shimar and Melki had descended only an hour earlier. Through the leaves they could see the hulking brutes using large metal dippers to fill the two big wooden barrels.

"I tell you, Yorg-Dogmah is fit to be tied." one of the soldiers was saying.

"Well who can blame him." his companion replied. "I wouldn't want to be in his shoes if we don't find that other moon dancer before the full moons."

"That's for sure." agreed the first. "It's not good for ones health to make Lord Salthazar angry. I hear that her boyfriend still insists that he knows nothing of her whereabouts in spite of our persuasion."

Shimar clapped a hand over her mouth to stifle a gasp. Melki mouthed the one word "Jonkin?" Shimar nodded briefly.

"Yeah, we even burned her village to the ground and hauled everyone that was still alive off to the slave pits, but no sign of the girl." one of the two Tephanites was saying. Noticing the stricken look on Shimar's face, Melki sympathetically reached out and held her hand.

"What does Salthazar want with the moon dancers anyway?" the other soldier asked.

"Oh, I don't know. Something about an ancient prophecy that is supposed to come true on the full moons." the brute replied with a shrug of his massive shoulders.

"What is taking you incompetent fools so long?" The shout came from the path above. The two froze momentarily, their big yellow eyes looking rounder than before.

"Coming right away." the two Tephanites called out as they hurriedly fastened the lids back on the water barrels. As they heaved themselves and the newly filled barrels back up the bank, a ring of keys dropped with a quiet plunk in the soft mud. The brutes were still talking as they rejoined the march, so they failed to notice that the keys were gone.

The procession was barely out of sight when Melki darted out and retrieved the ring of keys. By the time, Shimar had joined her she had rinsed the mud off in the stream and carefully dried them on her robe. She looked up and gave Shimar a shy smile.

"Maybe we can use these to set some captives free." she said.

"What! Are you out of your mind?!! Do you suggest we just march right into Salthazar's fortress in the forbidden desert?" Shimar was shocked at the audacity of the Myrondite girl. "What makes you think that the two of us can possibly succeed where many an army has failed?"

"I just thought that we didn't have much to lose by attempting it." Melki stammered. "With your people captured too, where else have we to go?"

"Since Salthazar seems to want me so badly, it doesn't seem wise to deliver myself into his hands. Wouldn't Salthazar's plans best be thwarted by staying out of his grasp, at least until after the full moons?" Shimar reasoned.

"Of course. You are right." Melki admitted with downcast eyes. "I had not considered that."

"For now I think we should find a good place to hide the keys. Who knows? We may yet have an opportunity to set some captives free." Shimar said, putting a reassuring arm across the other girl's shoulders.

Jonkin moaned as he regained consciousness. He hurt all over from the beatings the Tephanite soldiers had given him. Nightmare images clouded his mind, and his limbs were stiff and unresponsive. The cold dampness of the dungeon cell permeated his very bones. He gasped for air, choking on the oppressive blackness that surrounded him. The quiet and darkness pressed in on all sides. The only sound he could hear, apart from his own ragged breathing, was the steady drip of water that seemed bent on driving him to madness.

Was he imagining things or did his dull senses pick up another sound? Yes! There were definitely footsteps descending the stone staircase to the dungeon. He thought he could also detect a lessening of the darkness that enveloped him. Both the sound and light grew as the seconds passed. Were they coming to bring him food and water at last? A faint glimmer of hope began to stir in his breast.

How many days had he been imprisoned here? He had lost count. Down in this black hole time ceased to have meaning. When they threw him in here, there was a bucket half full of brackish water. This was now long gone. All he knew for sure was that it was the longest he had ever gone without food, and he was so parched that his swollen tongue stuck to the roof of his mouth.

An eternity passed before the heavy boot-clad feet reached the bottom of the stairs. The pounding in his head jumbled together with the tromping of the footsteps as they approached his cell. Jonkin squinted his eyes against the light from the Smokey torch that the guard was carrying. Jonkin's heart sank when he realized that the brute had brought no food or water with him. The guard rattled a large ring of keys, unlocked and opened the cell door, and pulled the young Crolarmite prisoner to his feet.

"Come with me. Lord Salthazar wishes to see you." the hulking Tephanite demanded with a snarl that showed his pointy yellow teeth.

"What does Salthazar want now?" Jonkin croaked in a raspy voice.

The brute did not reply. He simply grabbed hold of Jonkin's shoulder and propelled him forward, while Jonkin tried to make sense of what was going on.

Before they had confined him to this dank dark dungeon, they had tried to extract information from him. They had insisted that he tell them the whereabouts of Shimar. When he told them truthfully that he had no idea where she was, they did not believe him. During the torture that followed, and his subsequent imprisonment, one thought haunted Jonkin. Where was his beautiful, spirited Shimar? What could have happened to her? He simply had to survive and escape somehow so that he could find her.

Jonkin was in such a weakened state that the Tephanite guard had to practically drag him up three flights of stairs and along numerous corridors, until they came at last to the throne room of the dark Lord. Tantalizing odors assailed Jonkin's nostrils, and it registered on his dulled senses that a large dining table was loaded down with a feast.

"Come. Pull up a seat and join me. First we'll eat, then we'll talk." Salthazar invited with oily politeness. The dark Lord's skeletal features were frozen in a grimace that Jonkin supposed was trying to be a smile. Frankly, he didn't much care what the old creep was up to. Here was nourishment that he badly needed, and without hesitating, he dug in.

Most of the food was rather rich so Jonkin knew it would be wise not to overdo, especially after not eating for so long. He tried to go easy and eat slowly, but he was so ravenous that this proved to be impossible.

Unfortunately, the meal did not include the thing that Jonkin longed for most of all, a nice cup of cool clear water. The only beverage was wine in abundance. Because he was so hungry and thirsty, Jonkin drank too much wine, and ate too much and too fast. The result was that the room seemed to spin out of control. His head and stomach ached, and he felt ill.

"Now, if you have had enough to eat, perhaps we can discuss plans," Salthazar spoke with mock friendliness.

With a great effort, Jonkin raised his heavy head, and tried to focus his bleary eyes on his captor. Salthazar dabbed at his thin lips with a fancy cloth napkin, and then leaned intently towards Jonkin.

"We have found Shimar. I thought you should know." The dark Lord spoke in a conspiratorial whisper. "Unfortunately the news is not all good. You see she has fallen in with a bad crowd. These troublemakers are among my own slaves. They will have to be dealt with most severely. It would be such a shame if Shimar were to meet the same fate. She is merely misguided, while these evil doers, with their slick words, seek to destroy the peace of our world. They must be stopped at all costs."

"They must be stopped at all costs." Jonkin mechanically repeated the dark Lord's words. His eyes stared vacantly ahead.

"I'm glad you are in agreement. Now what I need you to do is infiltrate this group, and report their wicked schemes back to me. It is the only way for you to save Shimar from their clutches." Salthazar continued. "Go now and get me the information I seek."

"Yes Lord Salthazar." Jonkin droned as he rose from the table and stiffly exited the throne room.

Moon Dancers

☽ ● ☾

Chapter six:

THE PLEASANT WEATHER and the breathtaking scenery made the walk so enjoyable that Nordelia could almost forget about the Tephanites. Then she would catch a glimpse of the burn on Kendrig's handsome face and it would all come flooding back.

When the sun was high in the sky, they came to an enchanting meadow. The soft green carpet of grass was speckled with a wide variety of wild flowers, and the place radiated warmth and a sense of well being. Kendrig decided that they could all use a rest and some food, so they sprawled on the ground and took bread, cheese and smoked fish out of the packs that Greplog had provided for them. They had finished their picnic and drank the last of the water from their canteens when Kendrig spoke up.

"I think I hear a stream just up ahead. Why don't you three rest here while I go and fill the canteens?" he suggested. "It will feel good to soak my hands in the cold water."

Nordelia wanted to cry when she looked at the burns and blisters on his hands. Kendrig had paid a high price for their freedom. She hoped it would not be in vain. No one spoke for a moment. Finally, Bretlig broke the silence by endorsing Kendrig's plan with an enthusiastic "Good idea!" Though his tone was cheerful it seemed a little forced.

"I'll be back soon." Kendrig told them. Then he headed off with a smile and a wave of his hand.

Nordelia stretched out lazily on the grass beside the two boys and closed her eyes. She could hear the babble of the brook and the hum of insects as they buzzed in and out of the wild flowers. The grass felt so deliciously cool and inviting. She had not realized how tired she was until she lay down. The sun's warm rays caressed her body. A gentle breeze flowed softly over her, like velvet. Before long, she was sound asleep.

"Nordelia! Wake up!" Abuid's anxious voice demanded. "Kendrig isn't back yet and I'm getting worried."

"Didn't he just leave a few minutes ago?" Nordelia asked sleepily.

"No. You've been sleeping for ages." Bretlig informed her.

Nordelia sat bolt upright, wide-awake now. She shielded her eyes with her hand and gazed up at the sky. The sun had traveled far on its journey down towards the westward horizon, confirming Bretlig's words.

"What could be keeping him?" Nordelia asked, becoming alarmed.

"He probably fell asleep too." Bretlig commented calmly. "Do you want me to go and get him?"

"No!" Nordelia replied emphatically. "We will all go together. I don't want anyone else going missing."

They got to their feet and were just heading out when suddenly a most dazzling person appeared in front of them. His white hair formed a gleaming halo and his red eyes shone like rubies. His pale, translucent skin had a definite blue tint and his bare feet were immaculately clean. He wore a long shiny robe, and light seemed to radiate from him. His tall majestic bearing made him a most impressive sight.

"I am a messenger from the High King. I have been sent to guide you on your journey." a light musical voice informed them.

"Maybe you can help us. We were just on our way to find out what happened to.........." Nordelia began.

"You are looking for Kendrig. I know all about it, my gracious Nordelia." The strange being interrupted her with a dazzling smile.

"Hey! how do you know our names?" Bretlig blurted out. "And where is Kendrig?"

"I was just talking to Kendrig a few moments ago." replied the messenger, turning his winning smile on Bretlig. "He had fallen asleep by the stream and was just on his way back to you."

"See I told you!" Bretlig said smugly to Nordelia.

"I sent him off down the road to the south." The strange being seemed quite pleased with himself.

"But we were heading north. I am sure Greplog said the Prenelium city is up in the northern mountains." Abiud was puzzled.

"There are many ways to reach the Prenelium City. When traveling in the mountains the fastest way between two points is not always a straight line. The road twists and turns a lot. Like a river picking the easiest route it is constantly changing direction, but it is by far the faster and safest route." the stranger explained.

"But why didn't Kendrig come back for us before going off a different way?" Nordelia wanted to know.

"I must apologize. That is my fault, my good Nordelia. When I spoke with him, he was adamant about returning to you, stating how worried you would be. I told him of a fountain less than two lengths down the road, that has magical healing properties. Just think what it would do for the scars on his poor hands and face. He was still determined to come and get you first. He finally agreed reluctantly to follow my directions, but only after I assured him that I would fetch you all immediately, and send you right along. I just now left him. If you hurry, you can probably catch up with him. He will wait for you at the fountain, if you don't overtake him before he reaches it." the messenger told them as he led them to a winding road that headed south.

Before they knew what was happening, the stranger had vanished, and they found themselves hurrying south along the road he had shown them. They rounded each corner with the eager anticipation of seeing Kendrig on the road ahead of them, but each time they were disappointed. Just one more corner and then we will see him, Nordelia kept telling herself. With each disappointment, it was growing harder and harder to believe it. She could not shake the nagging feeling in the pit of her stomach that something was dreadfully wrong. She sensed that the others shared her misgivings, but they did not talk about it.

"Well I guess Kendrig had more of a head start than we realized." Bretlig spoke, trying to sound cheerful, but not quite pulling it off. "I'm sure he will be waiting for us at the fountain. Didn't the King's messenger say that it was only two lengths? We have been rushing along this road for ages. We must be almost there."

As the sun sank lower, so did their spirits. They slowed to a walk. At each bend of the road, they desperately hoped to see the fountain and Kendrig waiting for them. They continued along the road, for lack of a better plan, but their hearts weren't in it and their feet dragged. Twilight descended, making everything gray and shadowy.

They had almost stopped watching for it, when they rounded the corner and suddenly there it was. The fountain was an enormous stone basin, overshadowed with the statue of a giant bird of prey. Water spouted from the open beak into the basin, looking silver and sparkly in the dying rays of the sun. Nordelia could well believe that it was magical. It was magnificent!

Joyfully they ran up to the fountain calling out Kendrig's name. Their excitement soon died down for there was no answering call. No sign of Kendrig anywhere. Darkness was rapidly descending. Suddenly the huge bird of prey no longer appeared majestic. Indeed, it looked threatening, as if it were about to come to life and swoop down on them.

"Look, we don't know where Kendrig is." Bretlig stated in a poor attempt at a matter of fact tone of voice. "I don't know about you guys, but I'm thirsty!

Kendrig took our canteens to the stream with him, so why don't we have a drink from the fountain. It is supposed to be magical. Maybe it will help."

This seemed as good a plan as any, so the three of them bent over the basin and were about to scoop up water in their hands to drink when Abiud shouted, "Stop! Don't drink it!" Nordelia and Bretlig jumped back, then stared at Abiud with puzzled faces.

"Sorry to startle you, but I really don't think we should drink this water. If it is magical, I doubt very much that it is good magic." he explained. "As we were bending over to drink, I saw the statue reflected in the pool, and I remembered something that Greplog said. Lord Salthazar has a pair of huge stone statues of birds of prey just like this, on either side of the entrance to the slave pits."

"Are you sure?" Nordelia asked.

"Yes!" Abiud was adamant. "I remember Greplog commenting that a bird of prey was a rather fitting symbol for Salthazar."

"I have a sinking feeling that we have made a mess of things, and it's all my fault." Bretlig's voice was uncharacteristically quiet.

"No! It's my fault! Oh, why did we listen to that messenger? I knew I didn't feel right about Kendrig not coming back for us. I felt that something wasn't right. I was afraid that you two would think I was just being silly. Oh what are we going to do?" Nordelia wailed.

"I think we all had our doubts. I'm not sure why we were so willing to believe him, but I would not be surprised to learn that there was some magic involved." There was a calmness in Abuid's voice that he did not feel. "Whatever the case, it won't help us to sit around and blame ourselves. We need to decide what to do next."

"I think it is obvious that we are going the wrong way. Look where the sun is." Nordelia said, indicating the fast disappearing glow on the western horizon. "In spite of all the twists and turns, this road is taking us farther and farther south. How can we possibly get to the northern mountains by following it?"

"I agree. So, do we head back tonight or wait until morning?" Abuid pondered.

"I say the sooner we start back the better." Bretlig voiced his opinion. "We are all thirsty. It doesn't seem like a good idea to drink from the fountain. The next nearest water that we know about is the stream where Kendrig took our canteens."

"I vote to head back now, too." Nordelia spoke softly. "That statue is beginning to give me the creeps. The sooner we put some distance between the fountain and us, the happier I'll be."

"Let's go, then." Abiud nodded his approval. "It's a long way back to that brook."

They retraced their steps in silence, each lost in their own thoughts. Nordelia's mind kept going around in circles, wondering what had become of Kendrig, and thinking how thirsty she was. As she couldn't do anything about either one at the moment, she tried, without much success, to think about something else.

"It is funny how the more you try not to think about something, the more your mind dwells on it." she thought.

As they journeyed on in the increasing darkness, it became more and more difficult to see the road. They had to more or less feel their way along, which made for slow going. Suddenly they stopped dead in their tracks. They had all heard it. The sound of many marching feet approaching from the north. They could also hear cracks, like thunder, and low ghostly moans. The young Crolarmites lost no time diving into the bushes to hide. No sooner were they hidden, when the frightening procession rounded the corner.

It was a large troop of Tephanite soldiers, leading hundreds of Crolarmites and Myrondites off to the slave pits in the forbidden desert. The three watched helplessly from the bushes as Salthazar's men cracked their whips over the backs of their luckless captives. Nordelia found the pitiful moans of the people almost unbearable. Stumbling along, they struggled to stay on their feet, while chained together and driven so cruelly by the Tephanite brutes.

It seemed to take an eternity for the nightmarish parade to go by. They waited until it was well past and all was quiet before venturing out of their hiding spot. Nordelia breathed a sigh of relief, thinking how glad she was that it was finally over. Then she felt a stab of guilt. For those poor people the nightmare was far from being over; for them it was just beginning. Indeed it was not yet over for Bretlig, Abiud and Nordelia either. Three more times that night they had to dive for cover. Three more times they had to watch helplessly while the evil processions went by. They varied little in length; they were all long, far too long.

At dawn, they finally arrived at the stream where Kendrig had gone to fill the canteens. They knelt and drank until their thirst was quenched, then they began to search the area for signs of Kendrig's visit the previous day. A brief search produced the canteens, all four of them. Near by there were scuffmarks that could be signs of a struggle. They also spotted a crude arrow drawn in the dirt, pointing north.

"I think Kendrig is trying to tell us something." Nordelia exclaimed excitedly.

"Well it looks like we are to continue on the trail heading north that we were on before we got separated from Kendrig." Abiud concluded.

"Let's get going then." Bretlig suggested.

The brilliant blue sky and bright sunshine of the gorgeous autumn morning did much to lift their spirits. The horrors of the night before were all but forgotten. It even seemed possible that they would soon be reunited with Kendrig. They were on their way to the Prenellium City once again. They set off along the path with a vigor born of new hope.

A befuddled Draklog descended the dark stone stairs to the slave pits. His way was lit only by an occasional smoky torch, and a musty odor pervaded the confines of the stairwell. His meeting with Lord Salthazar had not gone well. His forehead wrinkled into a puzzled frown. How had it happened? He had gone to appear before the dark Lord, full of righteous indignation, prepared to demand that Salthazar explain himself. What was the idea of attacking his village and hauling everyone off here to the forbidden desert? Somehow, it had all got turned around so that he, Draklog, was to blame for it all. Lord Salthazar had voiced his disappointment regarding Draklog's failure to instigate a war with the Myrondites and explained how this had made it necessary for him to take matters into his own hands.

Draklog heaved a sigh and shook his massive head in an effort to clear his mind. At least Cleotisha and the other dancers were safe, and would remain so, as long as he cooperated. How had Salthazar managed to convey the threat without actually voicing it? At any rate, he now had a job to do. Apparently, one of the Myrondite slaves was becoming something of a troublemaker. Well, teaching one of those filthy vermin a lesson was a task he would relish.

The dungeons where the slaves were quartered whenever they were not working, were damp, dark and dismal. Nervously Draklog made his way down a gloomy corridor to the entrance of the slave pits. He was unable to control the feeling of dread that this place instilled in him, but at the same time he felt angry with himself for what he considered silly, childish fears. The heavy iron gates that marked the entrance creaked and groaned in protest as two burly Tephanite guards opened them to admit Draklog.

"So, where is this unworthy wretch of a Myrondite slave who dares to cause trouble? Where is the one they call Zebach? By the time I'm finished with him he won't be in any shape to cause any further problems." Draklog addressed the guards with more boldness than he felt. One of the guards completely ignored him. The other merely grunted something unintelligible and pointed to where a young Myrondite man was circulating among the other slaves, stopping to offer a word of comfort here, a helping hand there.

His appearance was unremarkable. He was of average stature and had rather ordinary features, but there was something about him that commanded attention. Draklog couldn't put his finger on it. There was a presence about this man, as if he were of far nobler blood than a mere Myrondite slave. At the same time there was a meekness that was far removed from the arrogance the upper class usually displayed.

What exactly was this fellow's crime? Draklog had not been told anything specific. The slaves certainly found something compelling about him. Could this be what Lord Salthazar was concerned about? Did he fear that this individual could incite the slaves to revolt? That was crazy! Draklog shook his head. There was no chance of a revolt succeeding. It would be suicide for the slaves to attempt anything so rash. As he drew nearer, he could hear this Zebach speaking to a young boy who was covered with many ugly scars and bruises, signs of multiple beatings.

"Don't be afraid. The kingdom of the High King is at hand. It is as close as your heart." here he placed his hand on the boys' chest to illustrate his point. He gave him a warm smile and announced "Your faith has healed you."

Immediately the bruises and scars vanished. Draklog was amazed and perplexed. How could this be? He knew that no Myrondite could do magic. What was this Charlatan trying to pull? Draklog had a chance to make a name for himself, and he could achieve a position of wealth and power even here in the slave pits. He was not about to let some lowlife Myrondite trickster stand in his way. He pounded a large fist into his open palm as he advanced. He had a job to do. He would do it quickly and thoroughly so that Salthazar would be pleased.

Chapter seven:

"A RE YOU SURE you know the way to this High King?" Shimar asked as the two girls hiked along through the alpine meadows.

"We will find him." Melki assured her with a determined look that dared Shimar to challenge the statement.

"I'm still not sure I want to find him," Shimar replied, "I only agreed to follow you along these rabbit trails through the mountains, because I think it is a good way to stay out of Salthazar's clutches."

"We will see." was all Melki said.

The trail began to descend and Shimar wondered again how, or even if, Melki knew that they were on the right path. After descending for about an hour, the trail leveled off and they found themselves in a meadow of tall grass. Majestic peaks rose like a wall all around, casting deep shadows. Shimar had the strange feeling that they were being held captive. As the sun disappeared behind the mountains, the temperature dropped rapidly. Shimar shivered and pulled her winter wrap more tightly around her slender frame. The cold wind felt like it was blowing right through her.

The two girls quickly found a spot to set up camp for the night and soon they had a small fire crackling cheerfully. They sat around the fire trying, not too successfully, to keep warm while they ate the few small pieces of stale bread and moldy cheese. the last of Shimar's provisions. A long mournful howl sounded in the distance sending shivers up Shimar's spine. The lonely reply echoed nearby. Shimar huddled closer to the flames, in an attempt to combat her fears as well as the cold. The eerie howls were repeated every few minutes filling Shimar with dread.

"Is it my imagination or are they getting closer each time?" Melki asked, her voice barely above a whisper. Before Shimar could reply, a threatening growl erupted right behind her. She whirled around to face the source of the frightening noise. She gulped for air and fought back the panic that threatened to overwhelm her as she looked into the two yellow eyes that shone in the darkness, just out of range of the fire. Slowly the shaggy green beast emerged from the blackness. A ridge of yellow spikes protruded from the animals backbone and saliva dripped from his large fangs. He paused, as if sizing them up, then repeated his deep rumbling growl.

Shimar noted with dismay that their unwanted visitor was not alone. Behind him, she could make out shadowy shapes and several pairs of glowing eyes just beyond the light of the campfire. Shimar didn't think the small fire would hold the creatures back for long. Indeed, the one who had ventured close looked as if he were about to attack. Melki, her brown eyes wide with fear, stood paralyzed. Out of sheer desperation, Shimar grabbed a dry branch from the small pile of fuel that they had gathered, and thrust one end into the fire. The leaves immediately burst into flames.

With a yell, she charged the beast, waving the fiery branch in his face. The creature snarled and backed off a few paces. Frantically, Melki followed Shimar's example. They couldn't venture far from the campfire. They were able to hold the snarling creatures at bay, but for how long? The meager amount of fuel the girls had managed to gather for their evening fire would not last long, and the ferocious animals that surrounded them showed no signs of leaving.

Shouts sounded in the north and they could see the lights from several torches approaching. Who could it be? Surely Tephanite soldiers would not be traversing these lonely mountains. The animals, that surrounded the girls, stopped their approach, and stared attentively in the direction of the sounds. Whoever it was, the shaggy beasts were taking notice. Moments later tall, hairy people encircled the two girls. Although they carried rather wicked looking weapons, they were not dressed like Tephanite soldiers. They did resemble Tephanites, but Shimar felt sure that they were not. They most certainly were not Salthazar's men.

At a gruff command from one, who seemed to be the leader of this company, the animals began to slink away, melting into the darkness. Was it possible that those shaggy creatures were under the command of these equally shaggy people?

"Look like we have sport!" announced one of the brutes, leering at the girls with a gap tooth smile.

"Come!" commanded another. Shimar and Melki had little choice but to go with these wild men. They were led north up a steep rocky path and through a narrow mountain pass. As they rounded a corner a huge galgabite fortress towered above them, causing Shimar to feel tiny and insignificant. It was much as she had imagined Salthazar's fortress to be like, except that the slave pits were in the southern desert, not in these northern mountains. Still, there was something most intimidating about this massive structure. A shiver went down Shimar's spine as they approached the entrance. A command was shouted, and those inside raised the iron porticos.

They were led across a courtyard, to what seemed to be the main building, and escorted inside. Shimar gratefully noticed a relief from the night chill. Furs covered the crude furnishings and were scattered about the flagstone floors as rugs. Stuffed animal heads adorned the walls, giving Shimar the creepy feeling that they were watching her. Three females dressed in shapeless leather garments tended supper. They chopped tubers and meat into a large black cauldron of liquid that bubbled cheerfully above the fire pit. The meager supper that the girls had eaten earlier had left Shimar feeling unsatisfied. The tantalizing smell of the meat and the tangy smell of onions cooking in the huge pot of soup made her stomach rumble.

As they were made to march their way down the length of the room, Shimar noticed a few older women sitting in a row along the wall busily sewing. They glanced up with interest as the group passed by them. A few children stopped in their rowdy play to gawk openly at the two girls as they were marched to a doorway at the far end of the long room. Here they entered a corridor lit by smoky torches mounted at intervals along the stonewalls. The long hall was lined by heavy wooden doors, all of them closed.

At the end of the hall was a large barred door with a guard posted in front of it. At their approach, he moved to unbolt the door and let them pass. They found themselves at the top of a winding flight of stairs. The girls hesitated, reluctant to descend the large stone steps into the blackness below. Shimar felt the sharp prod of a spear in her back. This was followed immediately by the guttural command "Go!" The girls were left with no choice but to obey.

The stairs were steep and dust and cobwebs stirred at their passage. The darkness was broken only by the glimmer of the sputtering torches carried by their captors. It seemed as if they were descending into the very bowels of Ku-Lammorah itself. Shimar had begun to wonder if the downward spiral of stairs would ever end when they finally arrived at a huge black cavern at the bottom. The feeble light from the torches did very little to dispel the deep darkness of the place. Instead, they only served to cast eerie shadows among the stalactites and stalagmites.

A large metal bolt was pulled back and a heavy barred door opened. The girls were shoved roughly into a small cell with a dirt floor. Two walls of the dungeon cell were made from iron bars while the uneven rock wall of the cavern formed the other two. Shimar immediately turned to face the hulking brutes who had taken them prisoner.

"Who are you people?" she demanded.

"We the clan." one of them told her, jabbing himself in the chest with one of his large knobby fingers. Was it a trick of the torch light, or did Melki's face turn pale at the words? Shimar knew she did not imagine the look of fear and revulsion that crossed her new friend's face.

"What are you going to do with us?" Melki bravely asked.

"Target practice." was the gruff reply. The heavy iron door was closed and the bolt shot home with a resounding clang that echoed ominously through the huge underground chamber. Without another word, the brutes turned and left. The echoes of their retreating footsteps died out as these wild men climbed back up the stairs leaving the girls in total darkness.

"Do you know these people?" Shimar questioned the Myrondite girl.

"I know of them. That is enough!" Melki's quiet reply did not disguise the contempt in her voice.

"Who in the name of the Prenellium City are they? Tell me what you know about them." Shimar's tone of voice left no room for argument.

"Hundreds of years ago Tephanites attacked the Myrondite settlements......... I know that has happened many times over the years..." Melki explained before Shimar could raise an objection. "but this particular time some of the Tephanite soldiers took a liking to some of the female captives, and took them for their wives. These Myrondite women bore them half-breed children."

"I didn't know that was even possible." Shimar was amazed. "Unfortunately, it is. These clan are their descendants. You may have noticed that these half-breeds are not very bright, but they are as strong and nasty as the Tephanites. Salthazar sent them away, refusing to have anything to do with them. You know how he hates flaws of any kind. They became outcasts, despised by Tephanites and Myrondites alike."

"So you're telling me this clan, or whatever they call themselves are half-breeds?" Shimar shook her head, although she was well aware that Melki could not see her in the blackness that surrounded them.

"Yes, at least that's how they started. They feel that everyone is against them so they mistrust and even hate anyone who isn't one of the clan." Melki's voice rose in panic, "They'll kill us for sure."

"We've got to do something." Shimar cried out, even though she had no idea what. "We can't just sit around here waiting to be slaughtered!"

"We'll never get out of here! We're going to die!" Melki sobbed hysterically.

Shimar could think of nothing to say to console the weeping Myrondite girl. Helplessly she patted Melki's back in an awkward attempt to offer comfort. Who was she to console someone? The more she thought about their situation, the more hopeless she began to feel. Finally, the pent up emotions of the last few days caught up with her. She tried to be brave, but she could no longer hold back the tears. She collapsed on the cold stone floor. Sobs racked her slender frame. In seconds, she felt Melki's arms around her. The two girls clung desperately to one another as they wept.

Neither of them noticed that the medallion Melki wore came undone and slipped off. Neither of them heard it fall with a soft plunk on the dirt floor of their prison.

Cleotisha paced restlessly in the tower room where she had been cloistered away with the other three moon dancers. She glanced at the three still forms in the beds. It was very early in the morning. Tonash, Jerah and Resha were still sleeping. Cleotisha could not help wondering what had become of Shimar. If she had been captured too, then why wasn't she with them? What did Salthazar want with the moon dancers anyway? It seemed obvious that he had some special plans for them; otherwise, they would be down in the slave pits with the rest of the captives. In a way, she would almost prefer it. At least then, she could be with Grandma Wenoch and see for herself that she was all right.

Cleotisha crossed to the one narrow window in the room and looked out. There really wasn't much to see. It was raining and everything appeared dark, dull and gray. She could barely even make out the thick stonewalls that surrounded Salthazar's fortress. She tossed her head of red curls impatiently. Oh how she hated it when there was nothing to do but sit around and wait.

Just then, an authoritative rap sounded at the door, followed immediately by the sound of keys in the lock. Cleotisha heard stirrings from the beds as the door opened to admit a burly Tephanite guard. A timid Myrondite slave girl entered behind him, bringing their breakfast. Her eyes were lowered shyly, refusing to meet Cleotisha's gaze. She placed the tray on a small table, and then slipped out quickly, and quietly.

"Out of bed you lazybones." the guard commanded with a cruel grin that showed off his pointed teeth. "Later the four of you are to appear before Lord Salthazar, so be sure to make yourselves presentable."

"What's this all about?" Cleotisha asked boldly.

"That's for Lord Salthazar to say." was the curt reply. The Tephanite guard turned on his heels and left, closing the door with a resounding slam.

As she stood staring at the closed door, Cleotisha could hear the keys locking them in once more. Perhaps now they would get some answers, she thought, as she turned to greet the other three moon dancers and join them for breakfast.

Shimar woke up to the light of a torch shining into their dungeon cell. Daylight never found its way down here so there was no way of knowing how long she had been sleeping. Melki appeared to be just waking up too. Two huge hairy men stood just outside the door. Their large pointed ears, sallow complexions, and round staring eyes reminded Shimar very much of the Tephanites.

One held the torch while the other carried a tray. On the tray was a large covered dish, a jug and two metal mugs. A guttural command "Eat!" was uttered as the cell door was unlocked and the tray handed to the girls.

"What is this? A last meal for the condemned?" Shimar asked testily.

"Too stormy for target practice today. You eat now!" one of the brutes responded, his bushy eyebrows knit together into a frown. Without another word he closed the cell and he and his companion turned and climbed back up the long flight of stairs, taking the light with them.

"Well, let's find out what they have brought us for breakfast. It smells good." Although she was trying to be cheerful, Melki's voice sounded small and frightened in the darkness following the departure of their burly captors.

"You go ahead and eat if you want to. I don't feel like it." Shimar grumbled.

"We need to eat to keep up our strength if we are to have any chance of escaping." Melki was adamant.

"Our chances of escape are exactly zero. Besides, how do we know the food hasn't been poisoned?" Shimar argued.

"Why would they poison the food? They want us for target practice, remember? Killing us off with poison would spoil all their fun." Melki said tersely.

"All right." Shimar gave in. "Let's see what they brought us." The two girls managed to uncover the dish in the dark, and felt inside. The dish contained small pastries that were filled with some spicy meat mixture and were surprisingly tasty. Shimar congratulated herself on filling the cups from the jug in the dark, and getting one of them safely into Melki's hands without spilling it everywhere. The water was tepid and stale but it served to quench their thirst.

"I don't believe it!" Melki exclaimed as a creak sounded in the darkness. "I just leaned against the door and it pushed open. They didn't lock it."

"You don't suppose they left it unlocked on purpose do you?" Shimar was suspicious. "I wouldn't put it past them to play some kind of cruel cat and mouse game."

"I don't know, but even if that's true, what have we got to lose by attempting an escape?" Melki responded.

"All right then! Let's go!" Shimar agreed. "Hold hands so we don't get separated. I just hope we can find the way in the dark."

The girls crept slowly, feeling their way along. Shimar had almost come to the conclusion that they had missed the stairs in the dark, when she heard the sounds of footsteps above.

A faint light of approaching torches revealed that they were not far off their mark. Quickly Shimar propelled Melki behind a nearby rock formation just as two of their captors descended the last stairs.

"Hurry. Get dishes. We go." one of the brutes grumbled.

"Prisoners not here.' His companion was puzzled.

"You not lock door. You let prisoners go." accused the first, pointing a gnarled finger right at the others bulbous nose.

"They not come up stairs." The brute shook his bushy head in bewilderment.

"They take underground tunnel. Quick! We catch." The two hurried off immediately. Shimar signaled to Melki and the two girls swiftly began to follow, keeping to the shadows but close enough for the torches held by the two wild men to light their way. Shimar was sure that this was better then going up the stairs and attempting to get past all the brutes up there without a clear plan. With any luck, these two would lead them right to another way out.

The brutes rushed headlong across the huge cavern and entered a tunnel on the far side. The girls were hard pressed to keep up, but at least their would-be captors showed no signs that they suspected they were being followed. Indeed, they appeared to be totally convinced that their escaped prisoners were in the tunnel somewhere ahead of them. The tunnel was full of twists and turns so sometimes the girls would be in almost total darkness till they rounded a corner and once again had the benefit of the faint glow of the two torches up ahead. Fortunately, the floor of the tunnel was sandy, so in spite of their hasty pursuit their footsteps made almost no sound.

After what seemed like hours, the two girls started to round a bend in the tunnel and saw that the brutes had stopped. Shimar knew they must be near the exit because she felt a slight breeze and could smell the fresh earthy smell of the outdoors when it rains. After the staleness of the underground, cavern, it felt good to breathe deeply. She could almost taste their freedom in the cool, clean air. They were too close to take a chance on blowing it now. Cautiously, the girls backed up a bit and looked for a place to hide. They hadn't noticed any side tunnels at all but just a little way back there was a small crevice in the wall of the tunnel. With a great deal of squirming, they, both managed to squeeze in. Shimar could hear low voices, talking in murmurs, but couldn't make out what was being said.

A few moments later the two wild men headed back down the tunnel the way they had come. As the brutes past the girls' hiding place, Shimar noticed that a third guard had joined them.

"They hide in cavern. I help look." the new arrival spoke authoritatively. Before long the three were well on their way back to the cavern where the girls had been imprisoned, leaving them once more in darkness. As soon as they felt it was safe they wriggled out of the crevice and headed towards the exit. After rounding a couple of corners, they could see a gray light up ahead.

"Be careful" Melki warned in a whisper. "They probably have a guard posted at the opening of the tunnel."

"I think they did but he joined our two friends to look for us back in the cavern." Shimar told her in an undertone. "You're right, though. We need to be cautious in case there is another one around."

All was quiet as the girls crept softly up to the exit. They came out onto a rocky ledge that was slippery and wet. They stood there for a moment, taking deep breaths and exalting in their freedom. The day was dark and gloomy, making it difficult to judge how late it was. The air was cold and the rain pelted the two girls as they stood shivering. In spite of this, their hearts were light as they began to make their way along the rocky path heading north.

Moon Dancers

☽ ● ☾

Chapter eight:

As Nordelia and her fellow travelers hiked up into the majestic peaks, they passed many streams that tumbled merrily down the mountainside. This gave them ample opportunities to fill their canteens and take long satisfying drinks of the cold, clear water. They picked ginkleberries along the way and rationed the supply in their packs. Still, their food seemed to be disappearing at an alarming rate.

The morning grew dark, as threatening black clouds filled the sky. The three Crolarmites trudged on, cold and clammy, through the drizzling rain. Suddenly the storm that had been brewing all morning broke upon them with unrelenting fury. The thunder boomed, the lightening crackled, and sleet pummeled them mercilessly. A harsh wind whipped cruelly against them, driving an icy rain before it.

The afternoon came and went without any sign of the storm letting up or of someplace where they might shelter from the bitter onslaught. They had little choice but to press on, in spite of the trail having turned to slippery mud, making footing treacherous.

Nordelia trudged wearily on, so numb that she could concentrate only on the act of putting one foot in front of the other. This became more and more difficult, as the sharp wind buffeted her from all sides, cutting through her soaked clothing, and chilling her to the bone.

She began to lag further behind the boys. A flash flood poured over the path, sweeping her off her feet. She was thrown face down in the mud, and barely managed to grab an outcropping of rock, narrowly saving her from being washed over the edge of a cliff. Desperately she cried out as she clung to the rock, hoping that Abiud or Bretlig could hear her above the gale. She was afraid to move, lest she be swept over the side. She helplessly watched the boys' backs disappearing up the trail. She had almost given up hope when Abiud chanced to look back and see his sister's predicament. He got Bretlig's attention, and the two rushed back to help her. They soon had her feet back on solid ground. She had already been soaked right through, but now she was caked in mud as well. In addition, she could now add several abrasions to her list of woes. In fact, as they pressed on through the storm, Nordelia felt absolutely wretched.

Presently they came to a small cave where they could gain shelter from the raging blast. It was decided that the first order of business was to get a fire started to dry themselves. This was easier said than done because there was only a small amount of wood on hand and it was damp. Presently they had a small fire going, but because of the damp wood it was very smoky and kept threatening to go out. They huddled miserably around the small sputtering flames in a vain attempt to warm themselves and dry their clothing. The smoke stung their eyes and made them cough. Their wet clothes steamed away but still seemed as damp as before. There was not enough fuel to keep the fire going long enough to dry their clothes, and the glowing coals did little to cheer them. As they sat around the dying embers they divided up two crusts of bread and a small amount of dried fish, the last of their provisions. The three Crolarmites waited out the storm, sitting cold, wet and miserable in the small cave, while the tempest raged outside.

Melki's medallion with its delicate braided chain rested in the large hairy hand of the clan guard who had discovered it in the cellar room where the girls had been held captive. This sacred Myrondite object had caught his eye as it glittered in the light of the torch. He felt extremely fortunate to have found such a valuable item, and was pondering how much he could get for it. Luck was with him. The merchant was due to arrive this very afternoon. Thinking of the storm that raged outside he hoped the trader would be able to make it through without any trouble.

The guard chuckled to himself as he pocketed the treasure. It should not be long before he could trade in the medallion for untold riches. At this pleasant thought, he rubbed his large knobby hands together in glee. A sly smile formed on his ugly face and underneath his shaggy eyebrows his eyes glittered with greed. He possessively patted the pocket that held his prize, then eagerly clumped up the long stairway from the dungeon.

Cleotisha stood with Jerah, Resha and Tonash in the dark forbidding throne room. Salthazar's thin claw like hands slowly and deliberately closed the large book that lay on his lap. He carefully lay the ancient volume down on a low table beside his throne, and turned his attention to the moon dancers.

"Ah, I see you are here. Good!" Salthazar spoke softly, giving them a grimace that was an attempt at a welcoming smile. "I do hope that you plan to be cooperative. It would be unfortunate if some accident were to befall any of your loved ones down in the slave pits." Here he gave a shrug of his thin shoulders as if to say that he really didn't care much one way or the other. Cleotisha noticed how pale her three friends appeared. Jerah was frowning. Resha's large brown eyes were brimming with tears. Tonash was biting her lip and she looked like she was about to cry.

"Look, we've already told you that we have no idea where Shimar is. I don't know what more we can say." Cleotisha said boldly. "In fact we would like some answers from you. Why did you bring us here? What do you want from us?"

Salthazar's face was a mask of fury. His red eyes narrowed to slits. His pale bony hands clutched the arms of his throne with a death grip. "It would be wise to take care how you address your Lord." he spoke slowly and quietly, enunciating each word carefully.

Just then, there was a crashing and banging just outside the door to the throne room. The Tephanite guard who stood by the door opened it to find out the cause of the commotion. Suddenly the air was filled with the sound of many beating wings as hundreds of white birds poured in through the open door almost knocking the startled guard off his feet. Salthazar ordered his guards to get rid of the pests. There was quite a commotion as the birds swooped about the huge throne, easily eluding the big clumsy Tephanite guards who pursued them. Some of the birds careened around Salthazar's throne sending him into a frenzy. He batted ineffectively at the offending birds with his long bony hands. The table beside the throne was overturned in the melee, dumping the contents onto the floor. The ancient book that Salthazar had been reading lay open on top of the small heap of rubble.

"Get these disgusting creatures away from me!" he screamed at his guards. Cleotisha could not help giggling at the ridiculous scene.

"Hey, those are Cordea!" she announced, noticing the yellow crest of feathers on the top of their heads. "Isn't it supposed to be good luck to see one?"

"If it is, then we must be in for a whole heap of good luck." Jerah commented. "There must be several hundred of them. I wonder where on Ku-Lammorah they all came from."

Just then, one of the birds landed on the open book that lay on the floor near the throne. With his sharp beak, he deftly ripped out a page, and then with a powerful flap of his wings he soared over the heads of the four moon dancers. When he was right above them, he let go of the paper and it fluttered to the floor beside Cleotisha. She had the feeling that the bird wanted her to read it. She dismissed the thought as silly, but there might be something important on that paper. She had to know. She quickly picked it up, folded it and tucked it into her pocket. She did not think Salthazar noticed. He was still too busy fending off the attacking birds to pay much attention to the moon dancers.

Two or three at a time the birds began to leave through the open door. Within a few moments, they were all gone. The only sign that they had ever been there were the overturned table and a few white feathers. Before long, a semblance of order was returned to the throne room. Salthazar glared at the girls as if they somehow were to blame for the rude intrusion of the Cordea.

"Make no mistake. I will have Shimar here before the moons are full, with or without your help. If you attempt to hinder me, not only will you fail, but I will see to it that you regret it. That is a promise." he hissed. "Take them back to the tower!" he ordered the nearby guards, dismissing them with a wave of his hand.

Nordelia and the boys spent the night in the cave, but slept little. The storm stopped sometime during the night, and morning found them little refreshed. They continued their journey with empty stomachs and clothes almost as damp as their spirits.

Even though the morning sun was now shining, a cold wind cut through Nordelia's clammy clothing like a knife, and hunger gnawed at her insides. She was so preoccupied with feeling sorry for herself that she almost didn't see the beautiful white bird with a yellow crest land near by.

"Look! it's a cordae!" Nordelia called out. "Isn't it rare to find them so high up in the mountains."

"I don't know, but he is one of the biggest ones I have ever seen." Bretlig commented. "I think they are called a royal bird because of the crown of yellow feathers on the top of their head."

"Maybe that is why it is supposed to be good luck to see one." suggested Abiud.

He doesn't seem to be a bit afraid of us." Nordelia observed. "It almost looks as if he is trying to tell us something."

"Don't be dumb!" Bretlig scoffed. "But I wonder if he might be tame. He might belong to someone who lives nearby. Maybe they would give us something to eat."

"Sounds nice, but very unlikely." Abiud voiced his opinion.

"He is a good size. I wonder if he would make good eating." Bretlig pondered.

"Bretlig! How could you suggest such a thing!" For some reason Nordelia felt quite ill at the thought.

"I doubt very much that he is as tame as he appears. The chances of us being able to catch him are pretty slim." Abiud surmised. Bretlig grumbled something under his breath. Nordelia knew that he did not like it when his ideas were not well received, and his empty stomach had put him in a surly mood.

"What does he have in his beak?" Nordelia inquired, noticing for the first time that the bird held something brown. They stood amazed as the bird waddled closer, deposited the object on the ground in front of them, and then flew away.

"Why, it's bread." Abiud observed as he picked it up.

"Maybe he does belong to someone nearby. Where else would he get this little crust of bread? He is known as the royal bird. You don't suppose that he belongs to the High King?" Nordelia wondered. "Maybe this is his way of providing food for us."

"This one measly little crust?" Bretlig was incredulous.

"Maybe it's his way of telling us not to give up?" Abiud suggested.

Quite suddenly, a shadow blocked the sun. The three Crolarmites gazed up with their hands shielding their eyes. Was another storm coming so soon? No. To their astonishment, it was a whole flock of cordea. There were not just a couple of dozen, or even a hundred or two, but thousands of them. The whole sky was full of them. The noise of all those beating wings was unbelievably loud. The stirring of the air was like a stiff breeze. Then, as if on cue, they all dropped a small piece of bread from their beaks. For a minute or two, it appeared to be snowing bread. All around the ground was covered several inches thick with little brown crusts of bread."

"Now I know this is from the King!" Nordelia proclaimed joyfully. "He really is taking care of us." She removed a couple of pieces of bread from her hair and popped them in her mouth. Food always tastes better when you are hungry, but she was not prepared for how delicious it was. This was without a doubt the best bread that she had ever eaten. She was about to comment on this to the boys but they were already busy picking up handfuls off the ground and cramming it into their mouths.

After they had all eaten their fill, they tucked as much as they could into their packs. By the time they had completed this task there was little left on the ground. What there was had become muddy and unappetizing. They shouldered their packs, and found that although they were full and bulky, they were surprisingly light.

The little group proceeded up the mountain path with new strength and Vigor. The bread seemed to give them more energy than normal food would have. There was something about it that put a spring in their step, making the difficult climb seem easy. Their spirits were also much improved. They laughed and joked with each other as they capered up the trail. The Prenelium City seemed so near, so reachable now. Nordelia could hardly wait to meet the King and his son.

In the late afternoon Shimar and Melki came to a place where a long rope bridge spanned a chasm. Melki informed Shimar that they had to cross it to get where they were going. The bridge looked old and seemed a little frayed in places. How long had it been there? Would it take their weight? Shimar felt a knot in her stomach as she saw the way it swayed in the wind. She peeked over the edge of the ravine and could hardly make out the bottom far below. She backed up a few steps, waves of nausea overcoming her.

Shimar could tell by the way Melki hesitated that she was nervous too. However, Melki rapidly put on a bold face and marched confidently up to the bridge. Beckoning with her hand, she called cheerfully, "Come on. Let's go."

"I think we had better cross one at a time. I don't know if the bridge will hold our combined weight." Shimar suggested apprehensively.

"Okay." Melki agreed with a shrug of her slender shoulders. "I'll wait for you on the other side."

"Be careful." cautioned Shimar.

"Don't worry." encouraged Melki "It'll be a breeze."

"That is one of the things that worries me." Shimar told her as she watched the bridge swaying from side to side.

"Sorry. That was a poor choice of words. At least it's not as bad as if I had said it would be a snap." Melki teased.

"Melki!" Shimar exclaimed in a horrified tone "Don't even joke about such a thing."

"You're really scared, aren't you?" Melki observed. "Try not to fret. It is said that the High King watches over all those who would journey to the Prenelium City."

"Enough talking!" Shimar spoke firmly "Let's just get across this thing."

"All right." Melki agreed. Without a backward glance, she started across. Shimar held her breath. It seemed to take an eternity for Melki to reach the other side. Shimar let out a big sigh of relief when she saw that her friend had reached the opposite cliff in one piece. Taking a deep breath Shimar determinedly approached the edge of the cliff. Her heart beat wildly as she stepped onto the bridge. She did not like the way it moved as if it were alive. She inched her way along, clinging to the guide ropes so hard that her knuckles turned white. Shimar tried not to look down or even think about how far below the canyon floor was. When she was out in the middle of the bridge, she did get a glimpse of the chasm's depths and felt instantly giddy and nauseous. She froze, unable to force herself to go any further.

"I can't do this!" She screamed. "I can't! I just can't do it!"

"Yes you can. Just don't look down. Focus on me, and concentrate on the act of putting one foot in front of the other." Melki called out from the far bank.

"I can't! I can't! I can't!" Shimar cried out in terror.

"You can make it! I know you can!" Melki encouraged. "You're more than halfway there. Keep coming and you will be safely over here before you know it."

Shimar took some deep breaths and fought the panic that consumed her. She stared straight ahead, trying desperately not to see the yawning depths of the ravine. It was a difficult struggle. It took all her willpower to force herself to take that next step. She resolutely continued to place one foot in front of the other, her attention focused on the opposite cliff where Melki waited patiently for her. Each time a gust of wind rocked the bridge it was a major struggle to keep going. Somehow, she was able to continue moving and, after what seemed like an eternity, she reached the safety of the far ledge. Her legs gave way and she collapsed breathlessly by Melki's feet, hugging the precious grassy slope. She lay there a few moments trying to catch her breath and calm her pounding heart.

"Shall we get moving? Or do you plan to worship at my feet all day?" Melki inquired with an amused grin.

"Don't be cute!" Shimar grumbled as she struggled to her feet. It sure felt good to feel solid ground under her feet once more.

Moon Dancers

☽ ● ☾

Chapter nine:

"WELL, THIS IS just great! It's written in some ancient language. I can't read it!" Cleotisha grumbled as the Moon dancers poured over the page that the bird had ripped out of the book. The soft, gray, morning light filtered in through the narrow window of the tower room, illuminating the four eager faces.

"Yes. It's obviously very old. It must have been written before it was decided that it would be better for trade if there was a common language everywhere." Jerah concluded. "Many years ago there used to be many tongues spoken throughout the land. Unfortunately, I don't know any of them. Do you really think what's on this paper could be important?"

"I know this sounds crazy. I have the strange feeling that the Cordea chose this particular page to rip out, and dropped it by us on purpose because there is something here that he wants us to read." Tonnash stammered sheepishly. She felt her cheeks flush hot with embarrassment. Now that she had actually voiced these nagging thoughts, they sounded ridiculous. She refused to meet the gaze of the other girls. She became intent on gently smoothing out the creases in the paper on the table in front of them.

"But how are we supposed to be able to read...." Cleotisha started to say when a timid knock sounded at the door. The little Myrondite slave girl who sometimes brought them their meals entered.

"I have just come to get your breakfast dishes." She spoke softly as she began to gather the bowls and mugs from the table. Her dark eyes fell on the page of ancient script that the moon dancers had been discussing.

"I didn't know you knew the old Myrondite language!" She exclaimed in surprise, picking up the piece of paper.

"We don't." Cleotisha told her.

"But I don't understand." The Myrondite girl stammered. "Where did you get this?"

"A little birdie gave it to us." Jerah quipped.

"A Cordea actually ripped it out of this book that Lord Salthazar was reading and dropped it at our feet." Resha explained to the confused slave girl. "Can you translate it for us?"

"I'm not sure. I might be able to read some of it anyway. Let me see." the

Myrondite girl said, holding the yellow page up to the light from the window in

order to get a better look at it.

"Please tell us what it says." Cleotisha said seriously. Resha just looked at Cleotisha with her solemn brown eyes and nodded her agreement. Cleotisha looked at Jerah inquiringly.

"Why not?" Jerah said without a great deal of enthusiasm. She shrugged her slender shoulders and added, "After all, what else do we have to do?"

"I'll do my best. This is an ancient prophesy." the slave girl said shyly then started reading aloud. "It shall come to pass on the day of the harvest festival... something, something.... moons are full.... It says something here about the moon dance and the sacred triangle, I can't quite make it out.......... the temporal and the eternal will embrace....... A mighty king will arise out of the branch of Nahor..........."

"What in the name of the Prenellium City is a Nahor?" Jerah interrupted. "I've never heard of that kind of tree before."

"He's not a what. Nahor is a famous person in Myrondite history. This king will be a descendent of his." the Myrondite girl patiently explained.

"Then why didn't they just say so?" Jerah grumbled.

"Shhh. I want to hear this." Cleotisha admonished.

"Let me see. Where was I? I think it says something about bringing justice to all the downtrodden and oppressed. I can't make out this next part.......... something, something...... appears that he has been defeated by the prince of the southern desert...... something, something....... deal this tyrant a crushing blow....... I don't believe it! Listen to this....... moon dancers will make sure the downfall of the southern prince......." The slave girl hesitated, her dark eyes wide with fear.

"What is it?" Cleotisha demanded.

"It is an ancient curse. I dare not repeat it." The Myrondite girl shook her head.

"A most powerful curse is pronounced against any who would harm the moon dancers...."

"Does it say anything else after the curse?" Resha asked, her brown eyes wide with wonder.

"Not much." the slave girl replied. Her eyes quickly skimming to the bottom of the page. "Let me see...... Light will conquer darkness. Peace will fill the Land ......Something, something.... The mighty king will reign forever and of his Kingdom, there will be no end....... That's all there is...."

"Do you suppose these things are going to happen now?" Resha wanted to know. The Myrondite girl nodded, her eyes shining with excitement, as she reverently set down the piece of paper. Just then a loud knock sounded. The door burst open, and a burly Tephanite guard entered.

Cleotisha stepped backwards, half-sitting, half leaning against the table in order to block the guard's view of the paper.

"Does it take you all day to gather a few dishes?" the brute shouted.

"I believe that this prophesy is about to be fulfilled." the slave girl whispered to the moon dancers "I must go now!"

With that, the Myrondite slave quickly scooped up the dishes and scurried from the room. The guard followed, closing and locking the door behind him. The four Crolarmite girls stared at the closed door in silence for a moment.

"Do you think it could be true? The moons will be full and in the shape of the sacred triangle in only a few days, and it is the time of the harvest festival." Tonnash pointed out nervously twirling her long dark curls with her fingers.

"The southern prince could be Salthazar.   That would explain why he wants us so bad. He is desperate to prevent this prophesy of his downfall from coming true." Jerah spoke up, becoming interested in spite of herself.

"Do you really think we will somehow help defeat him?" Resha wondered aloud, her forehead creased in concentration. "It just seems so unbelievable that anything we would do could make a difference."

"I know what you mean. It is hard to believe that we are important enough that someone wrote about us thousands of years ago. Could the prophesy really be talking about us?." Tonash spoke quietly.

"Oh, I don't know..... I think I could be one of them. Queen Jerah..." Jerah began to prance around the room with her nose in the air. She made an exaggerated sweep of her arm and called out in a loud voice "Slayer of evildoers, destroyer of empires."

"Oh shut-up!" demanded Cleotisha in an annoyed voice, "Can't you ever be serious?"

"Do you take this prophesy thing seriously? I mean how do we even know that the Myrondite girl translated it correctly?" Jerah retorted. "Even if she did it was probably just wishful thinking on the part of the fellow who wrote it. Most likely he just wrote what he would like to see happen and the harvest full moons seemed a likely time."

"I don't know. It seems like an awful lot of coincidences. I'd like to know who this mighty king could be." Cleotisha pondered, picking up the page and staring at it as if willing it to tell her.

"Wasn't it supposed to be written by some ancient Myrondite holy man or something?" Jerah asked, leaning forward and resting her elbows on the back of Cleotisha's' chair.

"The slave girl said that this Nahor was a Myrondite, so this mighty king must be a Myrondite king. It makes perfect sense to me for the author to choose a Myrondite king to be the hero of his story.

"Then why did he mention moon dancers in a positive light?" Resha wanted to know. "Myrondites hate us."

"Who knows?" Jerah replied. "It doesn't even tell us what these moon dancers do to defeat this southern prince." Here she withdrew from the others and flopped down on her bed with a frustrated sigh.

It was early but it already felt warm as Nordelia scrambled up an incredibly steep slope behind Bretlig and Abiud in the morning sunshine. Her arms and legs were becoming tired by the time she reached the crest where the boys waited for her. She stood up, dusted herself off and looked around. They were on a high narrow ridge that dropped away steeply behind them, and sloped away almost as steeply in front into what appeared to be a lush green valley far below. On the far side of the valley, there arose a majestic purple mountain, much higher even than the ridge on which they stood. On the glorious peak a golden city shone in the rosy morning light.

"The Prenellium City." Nordelia breathed in awe. Her heart swelled with joy. She felt like shouting for joy. At the same time, to do so felt like it would be wrong, like shouting in a temple or some sacred shrine.

As soon as the three young Crolarmites could bear to tear themselves away from the captivating sight, they started along the trail, which lead steeply downward. The footing was treacherous in spots, making their progress slower than they would have wished. As the morning progressed, it became overcast. Although it didn't actually rain, there was a chilly dampness to the air. The purple fog rolled in, obliterating the view, and making travel painfully slow. Nordelia grew irritable and impatient. She wondered how they were ever going to reach the Prenellium City at this rate. All day they journeyed down the mountainside towards the valley below. By late afternoon, the fog had begun to lift, and the trail wasn't as steep anymore so they were able to make better progress. The nearer they approached the bottom, however, the less like a lush green valley it appeared. The trail grew wet and muddy and a damp stagnant smell assailed their nostrils. By evening, there was no denying it. They were traveling through a swamp. Once more, they were reduced to a snails pace due to the poor conditions of the trail. Nordelia found slogging through the muck and mire, not only disgusting, but very tiring.

As darkness descended, there was not a decent dry place to be found where they might spend the night. Nordelia was bone weary but the thought of spending the night in the swamp terrified her. It was bad enough to have to travel through it in daylight when you could see if danger threatened. Nordelia shuddered, her imagination began to work overtime, transforming twisted roots into giant poisonous snakes poised to strike at any moment.

It was decided that the only sensible thing to do was to climb one of the enormous trees and shelter in its branches until daylight. Sleep did not come easily. The branches weren't terribly comfortable and Nordelia had the uneasy feeling that unless she were very careful she would roll out of the tree in the middle of the night. Each time she dozed off she would be startled awake by some animal noise rustling in the branches. The sounds seemed to come from everywhere. Instantly she would be wide-awake, her heart pounding, as she wondered what unseen terror was sneaking up on them under the cover of darkness.

Shimar and Melki huddled around a small fire for protection against the chilly night air. The purple fog that had hung around the mountaintops most of the day had descended upon them. It added a thickness that was almost tangible to the darkness of the night. Everything was still. Shimar had the eerie feeling that nothing existed outside the small circle of light from their meager campfire.

"How could I have lost my Medallion? It is very old and valuable." Melki sighed. "Oh, am I ever hungry! I sure wish we had something to eat."

"Well we don't. So quit complaining." Shimar snapped. She was finding it difficult enough to ignore the rumblings of her own stomach without a reminder. The girls fell into an uncomfortable silence. Shimar was about to suggest they try and get some sleep when a gravely voice spoke out of the mist.

"Would you be willing to share your fire with me? I haven't much but I would gladly share what supper I have with you."

At first they could not see the speaker because of the darkness and the fog. As Melki extended the invitation to join them, the shadowy form of a very old man appeared out of the swirling mist. He moved slowly, and with much effort, into the small circle of light around the campfire, leaning heavily on an intricately carved walking stick. His long white hair and wispy beard flowed down to his waist. The long black robe he wore hung limply on his thin frame.

His narrow face and hollow cheeks made his hooked nose appear even larger than it was. His snappy brown eyes held the wisdom of the ages, and his leathery brown face crinkled into a warm smile.

"I'm Shimar and this is Melki." Shimar introduced, remembering her manners.

"I am called Hushem." the old man told them. "Let's eat while we talk and become better aquatinted." Here he took a leather pouch from his belt and opened it. He took out a loaf of bread, a small block of cheese, and some dried fish. He pulled out a small dagger and sliced the cheese, then divided the food among the three of them. They all began to devour the supper hungrily. He also brought out a leather canteen containing water and passed it around. This was most welcome for the girls found that the meal had made them very thirsty.

"Could you possibly be the Hushem that is spoken of in the Myrondite temple?" Melki asked in awe.

"And just what tales have you heard about this person?" Hushem inquired suspiciously.

"Just that he is a Myrondite holy man, a prophet who prophesied Salthazar's downfall to his face. A very brave thing to do." Melki informed him.

"It may be bold, but it is also foolhardy to address Lord Salthazar like that." Shimar paused in eating long enough to voice her opinion.

"So you think me a fool?" Hushem cackled, obviously finding it tremendously amusing.

"Then you are Hushem, the prophet of the High King." Melki spoke softly, her voice full of awe. Shimar was speechless. She had no idea that this old man would actually claim to be the legendary person that Melki spoke of, and she did not know what to make of his reaction to her unintentional insult.

"Your friend here obviously has some doubts." the old Myrondite told Melki. Hushem then popped the last bite of his supper into his mouth, dusted the crumbs off himself, and then held out his hands to the warmth of the fire. Shimar felt his eyes on her as if challenging her to deny it. He seemed to expect a response from her, but she did not know what to say so she kept silent.

"What are you doing so far up in these mountains?" Melki inquired. "Are you journeying to the High King? Or perhaps you have just come from him."

"Suppose first you tell me what you two are doing way out here, without adequate provisions I might add." Hushem said, looking directly into Melki's eyes with a searching gaze.

"We are seeking the aid of the High King." Melki told him.

"Maybe you are seeking this High King of yours," Shimar put in "but I only came along in an effort to stay out of Lord Salthazar's clutches."

"And just what would that scoundrel want with the likes of you?" the old Myrondite chuckled.

"How should I know?" Shimar retorted "why should we answer your questions anyway?"

"I don't know what he wants with the Moon Dancers, but apparently he has already captured the other four." Melki told him.

"So you are the fifth moon dancer." Hushem glanced at Shimar, nodding his head knowingly. "Now things are beginning to make sense."

"Why did you have to open your big mouth?" Shimar spoke angrily, giving Melki a swat on the arm. "We have told him far too much already. How do we know he is to be trusted? He hasn't told us much about himself yet, has he?"

"Please forgive her impertinence. Being a Crolarmite, there are many things that she doesn't understand." Melki spoke apologetically. "In spite of that she really is a good sort. She helped me escape from the Tephanites and shared her food with me. Don't you see? That's why we ran out. She had not counted on being gone so long, or having to share her food with someone."

"Quit babbling like an idiot. Haven't you told him enough already?" an annoyed Shimar demanded.

"She is quite right, you know." Hushem told Melki with a smile. "You really are far too trusting. You know almost nothing about me, and have only my word that I am who I say I am." Here he turned to Shimar. "This may be difficult for you to believe, and I have no way of proving it is true, but the High King sent me to help you. Now that I know something of your story I am beginning to understand why."

Moon Dancers

☽ ● ☾

Chapter ten:

THE SHORT PLUMP merchant confidently approached the clan leader. He knew he had something that the massive figure on the throne wanted badly. The idiot who had sold it to him didn't know what he had. The brute had seemed quite satisfied with the modest price he was offered. The wily trader knew he was sure to get at least ten times what he had paid. A tidy little profit. He fingered Melki's medallion with it's intricately carved symbols and delicate chain. Yes, he knew this trinket was worth a great deal to the right buyer, someone who collects ancient Myrondite artifacts.

"I have something here that I think might be of interest to you." the merchant spoke boldly as he opened his hand to reveal his treasure. The leader of the clan stared incredulously at the item. Could this be the sign that they had been waiting for all these years? Were the old stories true? If so now was the time for action. Should they begin to make battle plans? Was now the time to attack their enemies? He must call the council of elders together at once. If the medallion was the one spoken of in the legends then it would make certain their victory. It had to be the one! Surely there couldn't be two medallions like this one. He must have it! Without haggling he gave the merchant the price he asked, and took possession of the treasure.

Long after the merchant had departed, the commander sat staring at the coveted item in his hand. Yes, now was the time to call a council of war.

He was becoming more and more sure of it. The coming battle would be spoken of for generations to come. Much blood was going to be shed, and he planned to see to it that it belonged to their enemies. As he heaved his bulk off the throne to go and summon his council, a cruel sneer appeared on his hideous countenance. The Tephanites in the forbidden desert would not know what hit them.

The next morning Nordelia and the boys were irritable, largely due to not having enough sleep. As they ate their special bread for breakfast, Bretlig grumbled and complained about the lack of variety in their diet. The day was cloudy with a continual drizzle of rain which did nothing to lift their spirits or improve their moods. It was a weary and grouchy group of travelers that set out after breakfast.

The trail grew steadily worse and more difficult to follow. They began to wonder if they had somehow left the right path and were following some side trail that was fast disappearing into the depth of the swamp. They struggled along as best they could, but the going was rough and painfully slow.

Nordelia, with her short legs, was especially having difficulty on the sinking, mucky trail. There were so many slippery roots and fallen trees that they were forced to clamber over. The boys often had to stop and wait for her to catch up to them.

"Can't you go any faster?" Bretlig cried out impatiently.

"I'm doing the best I can. Why don't you just keep your comments to yourself." Nordelia snapped back.

"I've heard enough from both of you, so be quiet!" Abiud demanded.

"Yeah? Who made you king?" Bretlig taunted. "Why should I listen to you?"

"Oh stop this bickering." Nordelia cried out in an irritated voice.

"Hey! What's that over there?" asked Abiud, pointing off to the left. Bretlig and Nordelia peered in the direction that Abiud indicated.

"Great Balogs! It looks like a road." Nordelia declared with amazement. She rubbed her eyes, and then blinked a couple of times, unable to believe what she was seeing.

"Look! It runs parallel to the trail we are on. It's heading the right direction." Bretlig pointed out excitedly.

"I wonder if it could be the real path." Abiud pondered. "We couldn't have strayed off the right track, could we?"

Getting to the road did not look like it would be any harder slogging than the path they had been on. If all was as it appeared, it would be well worth the effort to reach it. In their eagerness it wasn't long before they were close enough to tell that it was more then just a descent trail. It was an honest to goodness gravel road, going right through the middle of the swamp. What a welcome sight after trudging through the muck and the mire for so long. Joyfully they scrambled up the gravel bank onto the road. Oh the glory of being able to walk on ground that did not ooze and sink beneath the feet.

"I wonder who had this road built. Who would have the resources for such a project?" Bretlig pondered.

"I feel so weary that I don't even want to think about all the work involved." Nordelia shook her head.

"Why didn't Greplog tell us about this road?" Abiud brought up. "He knows so much it is hard to believe that he didn't know about it."

"Who knows? The important thing is that we found it. I bet it leads right to the gates of the Prenellium City." Bretlig concluded with a cheerful grin.

"It does seem to be going the right general direction..." Abiud spoke hesitantly.

"It's hard to tell for sure. You can't see very far because of the curves in the road."

"You don't sound convinced that this is the right path. What is it that is bothering you?" Nordelia wanted to know.

"Oh nothing really. I just have a vague feeling that all is not well." Abiud stammered, his face turning red in embarrassment. "I'm probably just being silly."

"Are we going to stand around here all day talking? Come on! Let's get going!" Bretlig spoke up impatiently. Nordelia looked at her brother inquiringly.

Abiud shrugged. Without further discussion they started down the road. It sure felt good to be on solid ground again. Nordelia began to wonder about the things that Abiud had said. Was it possible that this was not the correct path? She dismissed the nagging doubts because the truth was that even if she knew for certain that they were on the wrong road, she didn't have the heart or the energy to fight her way back through the swamp to the trail that they had left.

They had been traveling about two hours when the sky turned suddenly black. A cold wind whistled down the road, driving an icy rain before it.

"Not again" sighed Nordelia to herself as the storm broke upon them in unrelenting fury.

There was nowhere on the road to shelter from the raging elements. The three young people had no choice but to press on through the onslaught. Nordelia pulled her cloak tighter around her as the howling wind seemed to be determined to grab it from her. The thunder rumbled and crashed, echoing loudly from the surrounding mountains. The wind moaned and wailed like a whole army of ghosts. It was so loud that Nordelia would have put her hands over her ears if she didn't have to clutch her cloak so desperately.

The three Crolarmites rounded the corner and found themselves face to face with a large band of Tephanite soldiers, who were leading a huge procession of captives off to the slave pits. Nordelia had not heard the Tephanites approaching over the roar of the storm. She knew the boys had also had no warning. This time there was nowhere to hide, no time to escape.

Kendrig straightened up, pushed his blonde curls back and wiped the sweat off his brow with the back of his hand. He leaned forward, resting on the handle of his shovel. Hauling rocks and dirt was hard work. He knew that he didn't dare rest for long. Here in the slave pits you learned quickly that the Tephanite guards did not take kindly to any slave that dared to take a few minutes break during the long workday. Kendrig had seen more than one slave beaten unmercifully for what the Tephanite brutes called slacking off.

He glanced up at the massive stone battlements and towers that surrounded him on all sides. The walls were so high that he could barely make out the Tephanite guards against the background of gray sky. They reminded Kendrig of insects as they marched back and forth along the top of the wall. He knew they were unlikely to pay much attention to him. The Tephanites he really needed to be concerned about were the ones down here amongst the slaves. The two nearest guards were not looking in his direction. The others were far enough away that they were unlikely to notice him. Kendrig decided to take a moment to catch his breath before resuming his toil.

"Take heart my friend. The darkness of night will not last forever. Dawns golden light will come at last."

Kendrig whirled around to see who was addressing him. There, right behind him was a young man with the gentlest brown eyes that Kendrig had ever seen. At a glance, Kendrig could see that this Myrondite slave had been the victim of a recent beating.

"I'm surprised that you would even talk to me. Most Myrondites hate Crolarmites." Kendrig was puzzled.

He'd had very little contact with Myrondites prior to being brought to the slave pits, and the little that he'd had was not friendly. Here in the slave pits the Myrondite slaves far outnumbered any other race, and in the brief time since his arrival he had felt open hostility from most of them.

"Murder is against the law, but if you hate someone, haven't you already murdered them in your heart? Hate builds a worse prison than this one. My skin may be darker than yours, but it is what's on the inside that counts. By the way I am called Zebach." The young man greeted Kendrig with a warm smile. The two took their shovels and put their backs into digging while they continued to talk in undertones lest any of the guards take notice of them.

"My name is Kendrig........ Some of what you said is rather cryptic. Can you explain what you meant about dawn coming soon?"

"Do not be afraid. The time is at hand for captives to be set free." Zebach told him.

"Do you mean some of the slaves are planning a revolt?" Kendrig asked in a puzzled voice.

"Oh no. Nothing like that." Zebach grinned.

"Are you asking me to believe that the slaves, all of us, are magically going to be released?" Kendrig was incredulous.

"What I am asking is for you to trust me." Zebach spoke softly but earnestly. "Miracles do happen. That's different than magic. Magic is stolen power, but a miracle is like a gift for those who would dare to believe and receive it."

"If you two ladies are quite finished your gossip session, would you mind putting a little more effort into your work." The mocking voice of a Tephanite guard broke in. So intent had Kendrig been on the conversation and their digging that he had failed to notice the approach of the sneering brute. Kendrig and Zebach immediately stopped talking and turned their full attention and effort to their labor. Kendrig's back ached, and he felt dirty and sweaty all over. The muggy air was full of choking dust, making breathing difficult, but for some reason that Kendrig could not fathom, he was no longer discouraged. Instead he felt excited and hopeful, even though his circumstances hadn't changed. He still wasn't sure what to make of this Zebach fellow. So much that he said seemed so wonderfully strange and new. He had never met anyone before who talked like this man. Kendrig felt sure that there was more to this Myrondite then met the eye. At the very least, it appeared that he had made a new friend.

On her way to the brook, Shimar pushed aside low branches of shiny yellow leaves that drooped down from a large gumphalas tree. She could not believe that Hushem was actually proposing that they walk right into Salthazar's lair. What was with these Myrondites anyway? Did they have some kind of death wish or something? Shimar could see no good coming from journeying to Salthazar's' fortress deep in the forbidden desert. But what was she to do? Both Hushem and Melki seemed determined to go to the slave pits and set captives free. Hushem said that the High King himself had ordered it.

Apparently it was all in some ancient prophesy, that the moon dancers would be instrumental in defeating Salthazar and setting the captives free.

Shimar wondered if Salthazar knew of these writings. Could this perhaps be the reason that he wanted the moon dancers so desperately? Whatever the case, Melki and Hushem were adamant that she accompany them to the slave pits. She had tried to get them to see the futility of such a mission, but they just wouldn't listen to reason.

Shimar knelt on one of the moss-covered rocks that lined the little stream, and checked the fish trap that Hushem had constructed and placed there earlier. The water sparkled like silver in the sunlight, and felt cool and refreshing to her hands. Much to her delight there were five small fish inside the trap. At least they would not go hungry.

Swiftly and expertly she scooped up the fish and dispatched them. After replacing the trap to its proper position, she headed back to the small clearing where the other two were. She hoped they had been successful in getting the campfire going. These little fellows won't take long to cook, she thought, her mouth watering as she glanced down at the fish she carried. Yes, they would suffice for a meal.

As Shimar approached the clearing she heard raised voices, but could not make out any of what was being said. Melki and Hushem didn't talk to one another that way. The voices didn't sound like either of them, but who else could it be way out here in the middle of nowhere. As quietly as possible she crept up to where she could peek through the bushes. She thought it wise to remain hidden until she found out what was going on.

She noticed immediately that two strangers had joined Melki and Hushem. These two men appeared to be Myrondites, and Shimar did not care at all for the look of them. Both were dark and brooding in their expression and manner, as well as their complexion. The shorter one was thickly built, while the tall one was thin and angular. Shimar wondered who it was that he reminded her of. Of course! That disgusting little Eliphaz! In spite of being taller and darker, the Myrondite's pointy nose and chin, and especially his mannerisms, added to the resemblance that he bore to the weasely little Crolarmite. Instinctively Shimar felt that this man was not to be trusted.

"I thought I had made myself perfectly clear. Even if I knew where the moon dancer was at this exact moment, I most certainly would not tell you." Hushem spoke firmly, making no attempt to hide the irritation in his voice.

"I don't believe it! You would protect a worthless Crolarmite! Can you not see that by doing so, you are being a traitor to your own people!" the shorter, broader of the newcomers blustered. "Don't you realize how wealthy we could all be? Salthazar has offered a huge reward for her capture."

"Perhaps he doesn't want to share. Maybe he plans to keep the entire reward for himself." The other stranger spoke with an oily smile, and fake pleasantness.

"That is outrageous! Why in the name of the Prenellium City, would I wish to help Salthazar in one of his evil schemes?" Hushem sputtered.

"More to the point, why would you gentlemen wish to aid our ancient enemy?" Melki voice was polite, but she stared at the strangers suspiciously, daring them to deny it.

"I am insulted that you would dare say such things. Do you know who we are?" the stout little man blustered. The tall stranger gave his companion a warning look, and put a restraining hand on his shoulder, then turned back to Hushem.

"Let us not part with bad feelings. We are men of business. Just because we wish to make a profit, it in no way means that we support Salthazar." the tall one explained hastily. Although he spoke softly, his smile appeared forced.

"Be on your way! We would not help Salthazar, even if we could. Delude yourselves if you want to, but it is you two gentlemen who are the traitors to our people by going along with Salthazar's wicked schemes." Hushem accused, looking and sounding far grumpier than he had in the short time Shimar had known him. "I will have nothing to do with it!"

"Say what you will, despite our slight differences of opinion, we depart from you as brother Myrondites."

With that, the strangers politely took their leave, and quickly vanished from view. Shimar waited a few minutes to be sure they were gone, then stepped out from her hiding place and advanced into the clearing.

"Oh Shimar! I was so afraid that you would return while those two awful men were here." Melki said, seeming quite distraught.

"I did, and I got quite an earful." Shimar told her.

"I knew you had the good sense to stay out of sight until our visitors left." Hushem commended her "However I am concerned that we may not have seen the last those two. They seemed convinced that we know more than we are telling, and yet they gave up so easily. I fear they may sneak back later to spy on us."

"Oh, what are we going to do?" Melki asked in a worried tone.

"Another thing we must consider ....." Hushem said calmly, scratching his head in thought. "Way up here in the mountains we don't encounter many people, but we are sure to pass through more populated parts on our journey to the slave pits. There may be a number of others who would wish to cash in on the reward that Salthazar is offering. With her fair skin and blue eyes she is bound to stand out."

"Oh dear!" Melki put her hand up to her mouth, her dark eyes appearing even larger and rounder than usual. "I hadn't thought of that. People are sure to be curious about a Crolarmite traveling with two Myrondites."

"Yes. This is going to be more difficult than I had supposed." Hushem's forehead creased in concentration. "We must figure out how to avoid unwanted attention."

"I don't believe this! You two still plan to go to Lord Salthazar's fortress!" Shimar almost shouted in exasperation. "Do you really think we have any chance at all of succeeding?"

Hushem slowly turned and looked at her calmly with his deep brown eyes. He did not speak immediately but continued to stare intently at Shimar as if seeking some answer there.

"Do you suggest that we disobey the command of the High King?" he challenged.

"Please Shimar. You just have to come with us!" Melki pleaded. "It must be really important for the High King to send us there."

"Look, I don't even know this High King of yours. Why should I do what he says?" Shimar angrily spat the words out in an attempt to hide the fear she had about going to the forbidden desert. Melki looked hurt but Hushem was not fooled.

"Take courage my daughter." He spoke soothingly. "The High King will keep us safe. We have nothing to fear as long as we follow his instructions."

"I am not your daughter!" Shimar grumbled. "I suppose this High King of yours is going to supply food for the journey too."

"Of course!" Hushem smiled confidently. "I see that he has already provided tonight's supper." He looked pointedly at the fish that Shimar still held. She opened her mouth to protest, but suddenly felt too weary to argue further. With a sigh she sat heavily on a large rock.

"I give up! You two are impossible!" Shimar surrendered with a half-hearted smile. "It's obvious that you aren't going to let me get out of this. It doesn't look like I have much of a choice."

"Good! Now that that is settled, let us cook these up so we can eat! I'm starved." The old prophet grinned triumphantly.

They each took one of the long sticks that Hushem had sharpened on one end, and impaled a fish on the point. The chatter around the campfire took on a much more relaxed tone as they concentrated on roasting their fish over the open flames.

The golden glow of the setting sun filled the clearing with a peaceful sleepy feeling. With hot food in her stomach, and the cheerful warmth of the crackling fire, Shimar began to feel sleepy. She still dreaded the thought of going to the slave pits, but she didn't say anything to the others. It would serve no useful purpose, and it might just start the argument up again. Shimar was much too tired for that right now. She would sleep well tonight in spite of her worries. In fact she couldn't seem to concentrate on the plans that Melki and Hushem were discussing, and she was finding it increasingly difficult to keep her eyes open.

Moon Dancers

☽ ● ☾

Chapter eleven:

THE SUN WAS just peeking its head over the eastern mountains and had not yet had time to dispel the damp morning chill. Shimar and her companions eagerly picked handfuls of juicy ripe ginkleberries and popped them into their mouths.

Not much of a breakfast, Shimar thought, but at least they weren't starving. Without thinking, she raised a juice stained hand to rub an itch on her nose. A moment later Melki glanced up at her and immediately broke into a fit of laughter.

"You have berry juice on your nose." the Myrondite girl explained between giggles.

"Yeah? Look how brown the berries have made my hands!" Shimar replied, holding her hands up for inspection. "If it spreads much further I could get mistaken for a Myrondite."

"Of course! That's the answer!" Hushem shouted with glee. "Why didn't I think of that earlier. We must make you look like a Myrondite to avoid arousing suspicion in those we chance to meet."

"You want to disguise me as a Myrondite? How?" Shimar asked uncertainly.

"We'll start by staining your skin with berry juice to make it copper brown like ours. Some oil rubbed into your brown hair will make it darker, and Melki can braid it in a Myrondite style. I have an extra robe in my pack. It will likely be too short, but it will have to do until we can get one that fits better. The clothes you are wearing would immediately give you away as a Crolarmite."

They did as Hushem suggested, and Shimar's clothing was stored in Hushem's pack. The gray wool robe felt scratchy compared to the soft cotton that Shimar was used to wearing. It was faded and worn, and she thought it rather shapeless and unbecoming, but she kept her opinions to herself. Thankfully, it was clean although, as Hushem feared, noticeably short. It made Shimar feel like an awkward peasant child who had outgrown her clothing. She hoped that it would not raise too many eyebrows.

"Well what do you think? Will we get away with this?" Shimar asked as she pirouetted in front of the other two for their approval.

"As long as you walk normally, and don't prance around like a moon dancer." Melki laughed.

"You'll have to wear the hood up to hide the fact that your ears aren't pointed like ours. I can't think of anyway to hide those blue eyes of yours. " Hushem sounded worried. "If we meet anyone, you must keep your eyes downcast. Whatever you do, don't look anyone in the eye."

"How many Myrondites would hand me over to Salthazar for the reward? Are most Myrondites like you two, or like those two charmers we met yesterday?" Shimar wanted to know.

"You will find a wide variety among the Myrondites just as you do among your people, the Crolarmites." Hushem explained patiently "While Myrondites do not like Crolarmites, most would not turn you in to Salthazar no matter how high the reward. However, we must be extremely cautious. As with any people there are a few that are not to be trusted. Some, like those two sons of dust, will rationalize almost anything if the profit is big enough."

"Oh, this is just Great! It's bad enough having to travel to the forbidden desert wearing this get up..." Shimar ranted, indicating with a sweep of her hand, her juice-stained, sandal-clad feet sticking out too far beneath her robe. "But now you're telling me that I'll be in constant danger of discovery......"Melki came over and gently placed her hand on Shimar's arm. "Try not to worry. The High King is watching over us." The Myrondite girl spoke softly, but with such conviction that Shimar didn't have the heart to remind her that she didn't share her faith. Instead, she shrugged her slender shoulders, picked up her pack, and the three of them started their long trek south.

The setting sun cast long dark shadows among the tall walls and building in Salthazar's fortress. In the blackness under an archway, Eliphaz waited in silent impatience. He hugged himself, rubbing his hands up and down his arms to combat the chill in the air. Finally, he heard what he had been waiting for, the shuffling footsteps of his old friend.

"So good of you to come, Lord Draklog." Eliphaz's oily voice effused. It is good to have an ally of your power and influence in a place like this."

"So, what is this urgent business that you needed to see me about?" Draklog inquired impatiently.

"That Myrondite scum that you so aptly taught a lesson to, I believe his name is Zebach, is causing trouble again. Something must be done about him! He mustn't be allowed to interfere with your plans!" Eliphaz was adamant.

"Exactly what are this fellow's crimes? Salthazar was not clear about why he is such a problem. How is he interfering with what we are trying to do here?" Draklog scratched his head through his thick mane of red hair.

"Surely someone as wise and observant as you has noticed how he stirs up discontent among the people. He goes against the natural order of things with his so called healings and magic tricks. I tell you he is dangerous the way he goes about preaching his outrageous ideas. Unless we do something, and quickly, he will destroy everything you have worked so long and hard for." Eliphaz had worked himself up into a frenzy. His small arms gestured wildly and his narrow pointed face was red with fury.

"What is it that you are suggesting I do about him?" Draklog demanded.

"Surely someone of your influence can arrange to have him executed. After all he is only a Myrondite slave." wheedled Eliphaz, having regained a measure of control.

"Tell me more about him. What specifically is he doing that interferes with our schemes? If I am going to have a man destroyed, even a Myrondite slave, then I need to know why." Draklog spoke calmly.

"He is Myrondite scum!" Eliphaz spat in the sand at his feet to show his contempt. "Isn't that reason enough? Even most of the Myrondite leaders hate him. Surely you haven't fallen for his act."

"Of course not! Don't be an idiot!" Draklog bristled with indignation. "I merely want more information so that I can determine the best way to go about this. I can't ask Salthazar to execute him merely on my whim, even if he is just a slave. I mean, we have to have some kind of charge against him so that it at least appears legitimate."

"You are right as always, My Lord Draklog. Perhaps if you were to befriend him. You know, get on his good side so to speak, and find out what he's up to...... I'm sure you could come up with some charge against him that is worthy of the death sentence." suggested the small weasley man.

"Me befriend a Myrondite slave! Are you out of your mind!" Draklog Thundered.

"Oh it wouldn't have to be you, just someone that you could use your influence with." Eliphaz hastily amended. "I have heard that young Kendrig has become tight with that group. He would be the perfect choice for the instrument of Zebach's undoing."

"If he has fallen for that con artist's game why would he cooperate with us?" Draklog was skeptical.

"I'm sure that, if given the proper incentive he can be persuaded to become our little spy." Eliphaz suggested with a sickening laugh.

"Very well. I'll talk to Kendrig and see what I can do." Draklog's broad chest heaved with a big sigh. "I just wish things didn't have to get so complicated."

Kendrig pushed himself forward through the crowd of Myrondite slaves that had gathered near the huge stone fountain that dominated the center of the courtyard of Salthazar's fortress. He wanted to get a little closer so that he wouldn't miss anything. He could hardly wait to hear more of what Zebach had to say, although he found much of it strange and difficult to understand. In spite of the solemn atmosphere, Kendrig could feel an under current of expectancy.

"Cheer up, the time is at hand for your salvation. The High King has heard the cries of his people. He will come down and deliver you out of Salthazar's clutches." Zebach stood up on a stone bench in front of the fountain, his warm voice reverberated loud and clear over the multitude.

"What of those who are not his people?" a voice called out, and nearby several heads turned to look pointedly at Kendrig.

"It is not those who are born Myrondite that are his people, but those who love and obey him. It is he that follows the High King with his whole heart that is truly one of his." Zebach proclaimed boldly "Just being a Myrondite by birth in no way guarantees that you belong to the High King. How many of our leaders, claiming to be servants of the High King serve only themselves? Some have even gone over to the other side and secretly serve Salthazar while outwardly going through the motions of serving the High King."

"Do you accuse the leaders of treason?" a voice called out. Gasps and murmurs rippled through the crowd. Zebach raised his hand for silence and then continued.

"Although it saddens me to have to say it, there are some who deserve such charges. Rather that point fingers, however, I would ask that each person examine his own heart, and choose for himself who he will serve. If Salthazar is the rightful ruler then serve him, if the High King is the true and rightful King then serve him!"

"Hail the true King! Hail the High King and his Son." a voice cried out and the crowd erupted into cheers and shouts of "Hail the true King! Hail the High King and his Son."

"All right, break it up. Enough of this nonsense. It's time to go back to work now." the gruff voice of a Tephanite guard commanded. The crowd quickly dispersed as some of the guards employed their whips to enforce the order.

Kendrig shook his head as he picked up his shovel and returned to work. Zebach was sure not going to get very far accusing the Myrondite elders of being corrupt, even if it was true. Still, there was something about him; Kendrig could not help liking Zebach in spite of the outrageous things he said.

"You incompetent fool! Why didn't you arrest him while you had the opportunity?" Draklog berated the Tephanite guard before him. "There he was openly denouncing Salthazar, and you stand around like an idiot and do nothing."

"I put a stop to the meeting." the burly guard grumbled defensively.

"And did nothing to the upstart of a slave who started it all." Draklog spat on the ground to show his contempt.

"But I have never heard anyone talk the way this man does." mumbled the Tephanite, shaking his head in bewilderment.

"What is that supposed to mean? He should be executed for daring to question Lord Salthazar's right to rule!" Draklog bellowed in frustration.

"It wasn't what he said about Salthazar. It was the talk of the High King. I know nothing of the High King of whom he spoke. How is it I have never seen him?" asked the puzzled guard.

"You have never seen him because he does not exist. He is but a fairy tale for children and weak minded fools who aren't able to stand on their own two feet." Draklog sputtered, his face turning redder than his hair. "I'll go talk to Kendrig, maybe he'll be more reasonable that you." Turning on his heel, he spun around and stomped out of the room, leaving the Tephanite scratching his head.

Nordelia stumbled in the increasing darkness as she tried to keep up with the others. The iron shackles had made it difficult to walk, let alone move quickly. Nordelia knew that if she lagged at all she would be sure to feel the bite of the Tephanite whips on her back. A few of the soldiers had torches, but the small flickering light they produced didn't illuminate the way for anyone but those who carried them.

It seemed as if they had been traveling along at this shuffling pace for an eternity. All at once, they arrived at a familiar fountain. If anything, the stone lazigger statue, bathed in moonlight, looked even more menacing than Nordelia remembered. The Soldiers forced all the captives to drink from the fountain. Indeed, most were far too tired, weak and thirsty to resist. Nordelia and the others had little choice but to comply.

After drinking the fountains waters, Nordelia found her senses dulled. She ceased to care where they were or what was happening. As they continued their death march to the slave pits, time lost all meaning and whatever flicker of hope she had left died.

Cleotisha heard a loud scraping sound coming from the wall beside the door. What in the name of the Prenellium City could be making such a noise? With a motion of her hand, she beckoned the other three moon dancers over. Before she had a chance to speak, a small section of the wall slid back amid loud creaks and groans of protest. There, in a dark narrow passage behind the wall, stood a young Crolarmite man holding a torch in one hand, and gesturing wildly with the other for them to follow him.

"Who are you and what are you doing here?" Cleotisha blurted out.

"Shush!" The young man warned with a shake of his head of stringy dark hair. "My name is Ethan, but there isn't time to talk now. I have got to get you out of here. You are the Moon Dancers aren't you?"

"Yes, but why the urgency?" Jerah inquired. "I doubt very much that Lord Salthazar would dare to harm us."

"Perhaps not but with the festival only two days away..." Ethan left the rest of the sentence unsaid, and once more beckoned them to follow him. With a shrug of her slender shoulders, blonde Jerah stepped confidently into the narrow passage. Ethan, without waiting to see if the others were coming, turned around and started down the steep narrow stone steps of the secret passage that was so cleverly hidden inside the very walls of the tower. Tonash and Resha looked questioningly at Cleotisha who shrugged her shoulders.

The two followed Jerah hesitantly, as if unsure whether or not this was a good idea. Cleotisha had some doubts, but she was not about to stay in the tower room by herself. It appeared she had little choice, so she quietly took up the rear.

She was barely inside the passage when the entrance closed behind her with a definitive thud. As she carefully picked her way down the narrow stairwell, she felt the walls closing in on her. She couldn't see much of anything in the dim light of Ethan's torch. Her stomach fluttered with panic. She felt more trapped now than she ever had in the tower room.

Kendrig was restless. His mind was full of questions. There was so much that he didn't understand. During the short midday break, he sought out his friend, Zebach. Although talking to him often left Kendrig feeling more confused than ever, he could think of no one else who could answer his questions. Zebach was usually surrounded by his followers and often crowds of Myrondite slaves so Kendrig was happy to find his friend alone. Zebach was resting in the shade of the enormous stone walls munching on a crust of bread. He gave Kendrig a warm, welcoming smile and raised a hand in greeting. Kendrig plunked himself down in the sand beside his friend. He wrapped his arms around his knees and stared straight ahead, unsure how to begin.

"You aren't like any Myrondite that I have ever met. Who are you?" Kendrig asked after a moment of silence.

"Who do the other slaves say I am?" inquired Zebach with a mischievous twinkle in his brown eyes.

"My people either say you are some kind of sorcerer or magician or a con artist. Most of the Myrondites say you're a good man and a good teacher. Some think you are a prophet or Holy man. I've even heard some say that you are one of the ancient Myrondite prophets come back to life." Kendrig answered slowly, unsure how much he should say. A sideways glance at his friend told him that he needn't have worried. It was obvious that Zebach was well aware of the various opinions about him and wasn't bothered in the least.

"And what about you my friend? Who do you say that I am?" Zebach's face was earnest and his tone probing.

"There is something about you that goes beyond nobility. You speak with such authority. If I didn't know better I would say you are the King." Kendrig spoke the words with such a strong conviction that he surprised even himself. Where had such thoughts come from?

"You didn't get that idea from anything others told you." Zebach said, looking pleased.

Kendrig stared at his friend in astonishment. Was he claiming to be royalty? As if coming to a sudden decision, Zebach took a deep breath and announced in an urgent undertone. "Here is something I wish you to keep for me." He pulled out a medallion from where it lay hidden under his shirt then pulling it over his head placed it around Kendrig's neck. Kendrig couldn't believe his eyes.

The medallion and the chain it hung from were made from a translucent, almost transparent golden medal. The intricately carved piece that he held in his hands was warm to the touch. It had to be Prenellium. There was only one place it could have come from, and only one person that would possess such an item.

This was proof positive that Zebach was not an ordinary Myrondite. What could it all mean? Could it possibly be true? Was Zebach in fact the Prince, the Son of the High King? But what reason could he have to disguise himself as a Myrondite?

One thing for certain, he was not about to tell Draklog about this. He didn't like the subtle changes in attitude that he had observed in the big red-haired man since they had all been in the slave pits. He trusted Draklog even less now than when they were still back in their village. Kendrig wasn't sure what Draklog was up to or why he was so interested in Zebach, but the very fact he had been pumping Kendrig for information about his new friend was enough to make him suspicious.

"Tuck it inside your shirt as I did. It is best that no one see it until the time is right." Zebach's voice broke into Kendrig's thoughts and he immediately slid the wondrous object out of sight beneath his tunic.

Moon Dancers

))● ((

Chapter twelve:

SHIMAR NERVOUSLY KEPT her head down while being jostled from all sides as the three made their way through the bustling market place of a large Myrondite village. What would happen if someone were to notice her blue eyes? She was terrified to look up and worried that she might be separated from Melki and Hushem. How would she ever manage to find them again among the milling crowds with her eyes downcast? As it was, she found herself mumbling apologies to several people that she accidentally bumped into.

Hushem expertly wove through the crowd, stopping occasionally to purchase food from one of the stalls. Shimar could feel her stomach rumbling in anticipation of a good meal. They had eaten very little the last couple of days, so she was extremely hungry.

At last, Hushem lead the girls through to the other side of the market place. The crowds grew thinner as they approached the outskirts of the village. They were hurrying along, anxious to find a quiet place away from all the people where they could have a meal. In fact, they were so hungry that they could think of little else. So intent were they in looking for an appropriate site for their picnic that they failed to notice someone approaching them on his way into the market.

"Welcome! You three are strangers around here, aren't you?" the newcomer called out in a friendly voice as he neared them. Shimar froze. She did not dare look up to see what this stranger looked like although she felt a strong urge to do so.

"Yes, we are just passing through." Hushem informed him in a tone of voice that did not invite further questions.

"Where are you going in such a hurry?" the man persisted.

"You'll have to excuse us. We have urgent business to the south and are behind schedule as it is." Melki spoke politely in the hopes of not arousing the Stranger's suspicion.

"And who, might I ask, are the lovely ladies?" the Myrondite man asked pleasantly, not seeming to take the hints that his presence was not welcome. When this didn't bring an immediate response he asked "The tall one, is she promised?" An awkward silence followed in which Melki and Hushem exchanged glances, unsure what to say or do. Incredulous at the man's nerve, Shimar momentarily forgot the need for caution and looked up. His eyes widened in surprise as he looked into her blue eyes.

"We really must be on our way" Hushem hastily interjected pointing to the south and starting to head off with an air of urgency.

"I don't recall much in the way of villages in the south. Where exactly are you headed?" the man inquired, his eyes narrowing.

"The foothills." Hushem retorted, deliberately keeping the reference as vague as possible.

"And just what is it in the southern foothills that is of such great importance?" the stranger asked suspiciously, placing a restraining hand on the older man's sleeve. Hushem's forehead wrinkled until his bushy white eyebrows almost joined over his large hooked nose. His snappy brown eyes stared evenly into those of the stranger.

"We are on business for the High King, and you, sir, delay us with all these foolish questions. Kindly desist, step aside and allow us to continue our journey."

"I beg your pardon." The man grumbled an apology as they sidled around him. "I thought the King's messengers were a friendlier sort."

Shimar didn't look back, but she could feel his eyes on her back as they hurried on their way. They would have to travel a fair piece before they would feel it was safe to stop and eat.

Cleotisha shuddered as she unavoidably touched the clammy stone walls in the narrow secret passage. The musty, stale odor constantly assailed her nostrils so that she found herself reluctant to breathe. Her head felt dizzy, and her stomach churned uneasily. The queasiness and disturbing feelings grew as time marched on. It seemed like an eternity since they had left the tower room. Would this stuffy, smelly, slimy stairwell never end? The flickering torch that Ethan carried was the only light in the dark confined stairway. Bringing up the rear meant that she got the least amount of benefit from the small glow. In the shadows cast by her friends, she literally had to feel with her feet for the next step. The steep stone steps continued their unrelenting descent into the blackness below.

Finally, they came to the bottom of the stairway. The narrow passage went forward a short way, then ended abruptly with a solid stone wall. Cleotisha felt the panic rising up into her throat. She felt an almost uncontrollable urge to turn and run. For once, she was glad that she was in the back. If she had been where Ethan was, up against the wall in the cramped dead-end with the others crowding behind she would have felt trapped. Cleotisha wondered if she could have kept herself from clambering over the others to flee screaming up the steep stairs. As it was, she backed up a couple of steps and took a couple of deep breaths in an attempt to fight the panic that threatened to overwhelm her.

Cleotisha watched carefully to see what Ethan would do next. He reached the arm that held the torch higher, and looked up. "Ah, here they are!" He said pointing out a series of large metal spikes embedded in the wall. He then mounted the torch in a high bracket wall and started to ascend the wall.

"You expect us to climb up there?" Jerah's voice was incredulous.

"It's up to you. Do you want to get out of here or not?" he called over his shoulder without looking back. With obvious distaste Jerah grabbed onto the spikes, heaved herself up, and slowly began to scale the wall behind their rescuer. The two younger girls timidly followed suit. While Cleotisha waited her turn with growing dread, she kept her eye on Ethan until he disappeared above her.

Gathering her courage, Cleotisha began to climb up the wall behind her three friends. About fifteen feet up, she came to where the others waited for her on a dark wide ledge that ran along the top of the wall.

"Where do we go from here?" Jerah asked Ethan as Cleotisha pulled herself up to join the others on top of the wall.

"We go along this ledge and the secret passage continues just over to the right." Ethan explained. "I'm afraid that we will have to find it and traverse it in the dark. Sorry I had to leave the torch behind, but a person has to have both hands free to climb the wall. Oh well, it wouldn't have lasted much longer anyway." he added with a sigh, looking over the edge at the small, fading glow below.

"Quit babbling. Let's go. The sooner we get moving the sooner we'll be out of here." Cleotisha's voice was shrill with panic. The thought of being lost in narrow passageways in the dark was almost more than she could bear.

"Okay, everybody hold hands, and move slowly and carefully along the ledge to the right." Ethan ordered. The authority in his voice served to calm Cleotisha a little but her legs felt rooted to the spot. It took all her will to force them to inch along the top of the wall after the others. Soon they were in complete darkness, making their way through a narrow damp passage that seemed to go on forever.

Cleotisha was holding onto Resha's hand with such a death grip that she was surprised that the younger girl did not cry out in protest. Having to hold hands left them with no way to feel their way along the dark passage. Cleotisha's rising terror was such that she was no longer concerned about the minor scrapes and bruises from constantly bumping against the slimy stonewalls of the tunnel. Despite the offensive odors that pervaded the confines of the narrow passage, Cleotisha was concentrating on trying to take slow deep breaths to keep from hyperventilating.

Presently she noticed gratefully that the air seemed fresher. Shortly afterwards she could see a faint light up ahead. She hardly dared to hope. Was the nightmare really almost over? The dim glow grew as they approached, and Cleotisha saw that it came from the low roof of the tunnel. Ethan stopped right underneath it, took hold of a rope that hung down, and pulled himself up and through an opening. Cleotisha just had time to note that the illumination was from the moons shining through a hole in the ceiling of the passage when Ethan's head peeked over the edge. He reached his hand down to help Jerah who was already pulling herself up the rope.

Before long, all five of them stood on a rocky hillside below the slave pits. The fortress loomed over them, large and menacing in the moonlight. Cleotisha tried to calm her pounding heart and panting breaths, which she knew were not caused by the exertions of climbing up the rope. Ethan's finger touched his lips to indicate the necessity for silence. Quietly they followed him across the sand dunes with the three moons and the bright stars to light their way.

Shimar returned to the campfire after a brief trip to a nearby stream. It was amazing how a wash and a cool drink of water could refresh a person. Feeling much better, she began to arrange her blanket beside Melki's already prone form. From the other side of the campfire, Hushem's loud snores told her that he was fast asleep. Just as she had finished settling in, Melki sleepily turned towards her.

"Oh good! You're back. I was starting to worry."

"I was just getting a drink and washing up a bit." Shimar explained.

"You've washed off all the berry juice." Melki gasped. Shimar glanced down at her arms, noticing how pale they appeared in the moonlight.

"Oh No! I really blew it this time. I felt so sticky and dusty that I just didn't think." Shimar spoke apologetically.

"Well what's done is done." Melki said with a yawn. "Let's just hope we can find more ginkleberry bushes in the morning." With that, the two girls, weary from a hard day's journey, were soon fast asleep.

Nordelia barely registered the fact that they had arrived at the slave pits. Her back stung from the whips of the Tephanite brutes, her feet ached and the iron shackles bit cruelly into her swollen ankles. She was very exhausted and her mind felt fuzzy and unresponsive. The hours since their capture blurred together into an eternity of unrelenting misery. A hazy glow emulated from the sun as it attempted to break through the gray cloud cover. In fact, as Nordelia glanced around at the high stone walls that surrounded her, she felt as if her entire world had been colored gray.

A familiar noise hammered at her sluggish brain, clamoring for her attention. Feeling somewhat in a daze, she turned towards the sound. A tall broad shouldered young man was calling her. Where had she seen that blonde hair and square chin before? There were tears in his blue eyes as he embraced her. It finally penetrated her numbed senses that it was Kendrig, and he was talking to her.

"I had hoped you would be able to avoid the Tephanites, but I'm still awfully glad to see you. Where are Abiud and Bretlig?" he asked.

"They must be here somewhere. We were captured at the same time." Nordelia stated in a flat, unemotional voice.

"Oh, I see them!" Kendrig exclaimed, as he took Nordelia by the hand.

She allowed herself to be lead to where Abiud and Bretlig stood looking like the two lost, frightened little boys that they were. Kendrig hugged them and clapped them on the back. Bretlig's lower lip trembled and he looked suspiciously close to tears, but Abiud managed a weak, watery smile.

"I have so much to tell you! However, right now you must come with me. There is someone I want you all to meet." Kendrig told them cheerfully.

He led them to the fountain in the center of the courtyard where a large group of Myrondite slaves was gathered. A figure stood on one of the stone benches that surrounded the fountain as he addressed the crowd.

"A Myrondite! This is the important person you want us to meet?" Bretlig snorted in disgust.

"Hush! Just listen to him. We can talk about it later." Kendrig quietly but firmly commanded.

"Are you the one whose coming was foretold? Are you the son of Nahor?" One of the Myrondites asked the young man who stood on the stone bench facing the crowd.

"I am a descendent of Nahor, yes. The time is at hand for the prophesies that you refer to, to be fulfilled. You who stand here are about to see these things come to pass. I am he who will take captivity captive. My Father has willed it to be so."

"Who is your father? Do you mean Nahor?" someone called out.

"No, not Nahor, though he would be pleased for his hopes to come to fruition. No, the one I refer to is my Father the High King." Gasps and murmurs rippled throughout the crowd. Before this had a chance to subside, a voice called out.

"Hail to the true King! Hail to the High King and his Son!" The cry echoed repeatedly throughout the slave pits as the crowd cheered.

Nordelia noticed that Kendrig enthusiastically joined in the shouting and joyful hubbub that followed. Who was this Myrondite slave that everyone was so excited about? Why was Kendrig getting involved in all this Myrondite nonsense?

Nordelia felt confused and disoriented, and then her eyes chanced to meet two of the saddest brown eyes she had ever seen. The young man was still standing up on the bench while his eyes gazed deep into hers, as if he were looking into her very soul. She felt vulnerable, almost naked, but she could not look away.

With the entire crowd cheering him, she could not understand the source of his great sorrow. She began to feel that somehow she was responsible for his pain. But how could that be? She didn't even know him. Finally, emotionally drained and confused, she allowed Kendrig to lead her away to the slave barracks.

The desert dunes gradually gave way to forest glades and yellow wide spreading gumphalas trees. Cleotisha felt her spirits rise as the surroundings began to look more and more like home. Ethan continued to set such a brisk pace that the Moon Dancers were hard pressed to keep up.

"Stop running!" Cleotisha called out in desperation. "You're leaving us behind!"

"Keep quiet and try to keep up!" Ethan spat out as he turned to face them, his blue eyes glaring at them defiantly. "We are not out of danger yet!" He spun on his heels and to the girls' great chagrin he redoubled his pace.

Spurred on by fear, the moon dancers sped on after him. A worried frown creased Cleotisha's forehead. Weren't they safly out os Salthazar's clutches yet? This rescue had happened so quickly that Cleotisha felt she hadn't had time to think it all through. There was still so many unanswered questions. How had Ethan known of the secret passage? They still knew almost nothing about him. Why had their escape been so easy? Had it been too easy or was she just borrowing trouble?

Something about the whole thing just didn't feel right. The way they rushed along,Cleotisha felt she barely had time to breath, let alone think clearly. Presently, to her relief, Ethan slackened the pace a little.

"It's not much farther now." Ethan announced cheerfully, as he glanced back over his shoulders to see how the dancers were managing. "Sorry for pushing you so hard, but I think we are finally safe now. My village is just up ahead." Heartened by this news the Moon dancers kept up a brisk pace in spite of growing fatigue.

Moon Dancers

☽ ● ☾

Chapter thirteen:

Aᴅᴀʀᴋ ǫᴜɪᴇᴛɴᴇss ꜰᴇʟʟ over the slave quarters deep in the dungeons of Salthazar's fortress. A cold wet slime coated the stone walls, filling the blackness with a stale, moldy smell. The only sound to be heard was the rhythmic dripping of water somewhere nearby. The small flickering glow of a single candle illuminated the faces of the small group of slaves gathered.

All eyes focused on Zebach as he drew out the items from inside his cloak. First, he laid a pair of shears on the small wooden table in front of him, followed by three rolls of ribbon: One red, one white and one gold.

"The red cord is a symbol of my blood that will soon be shed for you, the white stands for the pure clean heart that will result for those who apply my sacrifice to themselves. The gold represents my coming kingdom. It is the promise of my return."

Zebach proceeded to cut lengths of the ribbon, and braiding the three colors together, he formed a bracelet for each one there. "Wear these in remembrance of me.," his words echoed in the silence that had fallen over the group as he handed out the bracelets.

Glancing around at the faces in the soft illumination of the candle, Kendrig's eyes met Jonkin's. Kendrig smiled encouragingly. It was good to have an old friend as part of this special group of new friends. Jonkin seemed subtly changed after his experience in Salthazar's dungeon. Kendrig was not sure what to make of it, but it would not do any good to worry, so he shrugged it off.

Now, looking at Jonkin's thoughtful expression, Kendrig was sure that he was not the only one puzzled by what Zebach had said. Yet, no one dared ask him what he meant. To do so would have seemed almost blasphemous. Although they didn't understand what it was all about, they all sensed that this moment was sacred and holy.

Salthazar's throne room was as deathly still as a giant tomb. The dark Lord himself sat motionless, a pale statue, his thin claw like hands resting on the arms of the throne. Draklog stood before him, nervously shuffling his large feet. He cleared his throat. The sound echoed loudly in the quiet hall causing the red giant to cringe.

"Well, what is it this time?" Salthazar asked in a low voice that was full of irritation and annoyance. His red eyes narrowed to slits, and his thin lips barley moved as he spoke.

"It is about that slave Zebach....." Draklog began hesitantly.

"Speak up! What about him?" The bony figure on the throne spat out impatiently.

"He is causing problems again, my Lord. I really think he should be executed." the big Crolarmite blurted out.

"And just how did you come to that brilliant conclusion? Do you think yourself better able to judge such things than I?" Salthazar laughed derisively.

"But he questions your right to rule, my Lord. He fills the people's heads with nonsense about the High King delivering them. He is trouble I tell you!" Draklog blurted out.

"Is that so? Then why haven't you dealt with him?" Salthazar leaned forward, fixing his piercing red eyes on Draklog as he waited for an answer.

"I thought to inform my Lord first........ to see how you wanted it to be........handled." stammered Draklog, backing up a couple of steps.

"Yes, these things must be done carefully. We can't have him become a martyr for the slaves to rally around." Salthazar sat back. His bony hand stroked his chin thoughtfully. "We have a spy in place, ready to betray him. It should not be too difficult to incite his own people against him so that they cry out, demanding his death."

"Many of the Myrondite religious leaders are already opposed to him. Perhaps we could enlist their aid." Draklog suggested hesitantly.

"Very good. See to it and the sooner the better." The dark figure on the throne announced with an air of finality.

Taking the hint that he was dismissed, Draklog gave a low bow, then turned and marched briskly from the throne room.

A frown creased Salthazar's ghostly brow. "Could it possibly be him?" he muttered in an undertone, his thin lips barely moving. His long bony fingers grasped the scepter fiercely, his red eyes burned as he stared at the door where Draklog had left.

Cleotisha paced back and forth in the bedroom of the small cottage, trying to sort out her troubled thoughts. She should feel a measure of peace now that she was safely in a Crolarmite village. Then why did she feel so ill at ease?

The other three girls were fast asleep, exhausted from their arduous escape. What was wrong with her? Why couldn't she follow their wise example? She could clearly make out the sleeping forms of the other moon dancers in the silvery light of the moons that streamed through the window. The only sound she could hear, the gentle even breathing of her friends, seemed loud in the stillness of the night.

The sea must be as calm as glass tonight for she couldn't make out the pounding beat of the waves on the shore. She could not even hear any of the normal night sounds like the buzzing insects or the croaking of the little red fire frogs. Why did the silence seem so oppressive and ominous, even frightening?

She must get a grip on herself. She mustn't let her imagination run away with her. Why was she still so suspicious of Ethan? After all, he had rescued them from Salthazar, hadn't he? But how had he known about the secret passage way? He had still not given them any answers. Indeed, he had interrogated them. He had been visibly upset when they explained that they didn't know where Shimar was, nor did they know what had become of her replacement, Nordelia.

Why did his reaction bother her so much? Wasn't it only natural that he would be very disappointed when he had been so hoping that they would be able to hold the moon festival tomorrow night after all? Or was there more to it than that?

She had not told her friends about her fears and doubts. Jerah would think she was just being silly, and she would probably be right. Tonash and Resha were easily frightened. Why upset the two younger girls when her worries were most likely unfounded? Then why couldn't she shake the feeling that some nameless danger threatened? Cleotisha shuddered, feeling suddenly cold. With a sigh, she crawled under the blankets of the empty cot and tried to will herself to sleep.

"What is this vitally important mission that Hushem has gone to do for the High King?" Shimar asked grumpily as she pulled her blanket more tightly around her in an attempt to ward off the cold night air. The glow from the remains of the small campfire reflected in Melki's liquidy brown eyes.

"I don't know any more about it than you do." she answered wearily.

"So he didn't tell you either." Shimar said with a touch of irritation.

"No he didn't. Now quit talking and go to sleep." commanded Melki. She then curled up in her blanket with her back to Shimar in order to forestall further conversation.

Shimar, feeling slightly miffed at being spoken to like a child, turned her back to Melki and the fire. She would sleep when she chose to and not before. She sat there on the sandy ground with her arms around her knees and her blanket draped around her shoulders like a cloak. Her gaze was drawn instinctively heavenward.

The night sky was dominated by the three moons that formed the points of a perfect triangle. Shimar felt a stab of pain in her heart at the realization that tomorrow night was the harvest full moons, the night of the sacred moon festival. Only this year there would be no celebration. This year there would be no moon dance. A tear rolled down her cheek, and she angrily brushed it away with the back of her hand. How silly to grieve over such things when there were far more serious problems to worry about.

The silvery light of the moons illuminated the countryside making it appear enchanted. Not that there was much to see except rolling grassy hills and shifting shadows. Suddenly, Shimar was jarred out of her brooding thoughts, all her senses alert. She distinctly heard a cough, and it did not come from where Melki lay curled up on the ground behind her. Her eyes searched the spot on the slopes below where she had heard the sound. Was there really movement down in that hollow amongst the shadows? Or could she have just imagined it? No, she was sure that there was something there, and whatever it was, it seemed to be making its way up the hill, heading right towards them.

Cleotisha heard a scraping sound at the door of the cabin. As she watched, the door creaked open and a cloaked figure crept stealthily into the bedroom. She quickly removed the cover from the brineconc lamp by the bed, and instantly the room was flooded with light. Jerah groaned in protest as she sat up squinting against the sudden brightness.

The other dancers woke too, shielding their eyes with their hands, and trying to figure out what was happening. There, standing before them, was a thin, strange looking little brown man, with pointed ears, a large hooked nose, and a long wispy white beard.

"Who are you, and what are you doing here?" Cleotisha demanded.

"My name is Hushem. You are in grave danger, I have come to get you out of here." the old man spoke urgently.

"Don't trust him! Can't you see that he is a Myrondite?" Jerah blurted out. Resha's brown eyes grew wide with fear, and Tonash's lower lip began to tremble as she fought back tears.

"You don't understand. The High King has sent me to fetch you. I have just come from Shimar and Melki. I can take you to them. We must go at once! You are in grave danger here." Hushem repeated earnestly.

"Who is Melki? What danger? We are in a Crolarmite village." Jerah snorted, arrogantly tossing her head of blonde curls.

"We don't know any Melki or this High King you speak of. Why should we believe you?" Cleotisha asked "How do we know that you aren't the one responsible for Shimar's disappearance?"

"I can think of no good reason for you to trust me, but you have got to understand. Just because it is a Crolarmite village in no way makes it safe. This particular village is completely sold out to Salthazar. You have not escaped his clutches at all. This is a deception designed to flush out Shimar. He wants all five of you, and his plans for you are not good." Hushem rambled, desperately trying to get them to listen to him. "It is the full moons tomorrow. We must get you out of here now, tonight!"

"I'm not sure why, but I believe you." Cleotisha spoke calmly "You say you know where Shimar is?"

"I'll take you to her at once." Hushem breathed a sigh of relief.

"Wait a minute. Who said we are going anywhere with you." Jerah turned to Cleotisha and demanded. "Have you lost your mind? Are you actually suggesting that we go off with this....this... Myrondite?"

"I'm not sure what I'm suggesting. All I know is that I do not feel safe here in this village. Something has not felt right about this rescue from the beginning." Cleotisha paused, wrestling with a difficult decision, then with firm resolve she stepped closer to the old Myrondite and announced. "Look, you do what you think is right. I know this sounds crazy, but I'm going with him."

The moon dancers stood looking at each other for a moment that seemed to stretch to eternity. Slowly Tonash and Resha crossed the room and stood beside Cleotisha and Hushem. Jerah glared at them, but finally, with a resigned sigh, she joined the others.

"Well, if we are going, we had better get started. Oh, and you had better cover the lamp again before somebody notices the light." she suggested. In less than a minute they were slipping out of the village like five silent shadows.

Melki woke suddenly to find a cold hand clasped firmly over her mouth. She struggled and kicked, scratched and even bit the hand that restrained her. Finally, a familiar voice began to penetrate her consciousness.

"It's me you idiot! Now stop fighting like a Sarconian wildcat, and listen," Shimar's urgent whisper hissed in Melki's' ear. "Someone or something is coming up the hill towards us. Hurry, we've got to hide!"

Melki looked around at the grassy hillside in disbelief. Just where was Shimar suggesting that they hide? For that matter, just where was this danger that had her usually levelheaded friend in such a frantic state. She was about to tell Shimar that she was imagining things when she spotted a mass of large shadowy forms approaching silently.

"There's nowhere to hide. What are we going to do?" Shimar's voice was shrill with panic.

"Shush!" warned Melki in an undertone. "Maybe if we just lie down flat in the tall grass and keep quiet they won't see us."

Swiftly they followed Melki's suggestion. Then came the waiting. The minutes ticked by, each one an eternity. The only sound that came to Melki's ears was a slight rustling. Was it just the wind? She dared not move a muscle. From her prone position she peered between the long blades of grass trying to see what was happening. She was almost sure she detected some movement in the little clearing where the remains of the campfire smoldered.

Suddenly she heard footsteps and there only inches in front of her face stood a pair of enormous boot clad feet. Could it be a Tephanite soldier?

"They not here." a voice announced, sounding annoyed.

"Fire still warm. They not go far." a reply came from beside the stone ring that contained the glowing embers. "Come, we look."

A brief search quickly produced the two frightened girls. Melki and Shimar found themselves in the midst of a troop of clan warriors. What would become of them now? What in the name of the Prenellium City were the clan doing down in these southern foothills?

Almost as if he could read her mind, the gruff voice of one of the hulking brutes penetrated Melki's anxious thoughts. "We attack Tephanite fortress. Big battle soon. Maybe use you as target practice...." Whatever else he might have said was silenced with a cuff across the mouth by the commander of the clan army.

"You not know what prophesy say?" here the commander paused before going on, as if struggling to remember the exact words. "Two girls come to solve clan's plight. One is brown, the other white. One of day, one of night. They aid the clan and put things right. Time has come to release its might. Now the clan will win the fight."

"How we win? Leader prisoner in tower." one of the warriors spoke up.

"That how girls help us." the commander insisted. "They rescue leader. Then he raise porticos, let army into fortress."

"What makes you think we'll help you?" Shimar asked testily.

"You have friends and family who are prisoner in fortress. We your best chance to rescue them." The commander said with confidence. "We make plans in morning. Now we rest."

With that, the warriors sprawled on the ground right where they were. Soon the night air filled with the loud rumble of their snoring. Melki and Shimar looked at each other, wondering what to do. The chances of sneaking through the sleeping brutes without getting caught was extremely unlikely. Suppose what the commander said was true? Did they even want to escape? Maybe helping the clan was the only way to free their loved ones who were prisoners. However, could the Clan be trusted?

Moon Dancers

)) ● ((

Chapter fourteen:

Dawn was just beginning to stretch its silver fingers across the Eastern sky. Draklog stood in the shadow of the doorway leaning on the heavy wooden door that lead to the guards' room. His arms were folded across his huge barrel chest, and his brow furrowed deep in thought. The animated approach of Eliphaz succeeded in capturing his attention. The small man rushed towards him, robes flapping in the wind, obviously bearing good news.

"Well done, Lord Draklog." Eliphaz commented in an oily voice. "You did it! It has all been arranged. He is to be executed today."

"Good! Then we will not have to worry about him interfering. It helped having a traitor in their midst." Draklog nodded with a satisfied smile.

"Yes, everything is going according to plan. It won't be long now until we can enjoy the fruits of our labor." The greasy little man rubbed his hands together with glee.

Shimar could not believe what had happened. Here she and Melki were in the midst of the clan army that had crept up the hill the previous night, and yet she was not frightened or even worried. She was unsure how it had happened, but somehow these hulking brutes had become their friends.

As it turned out, it was a blessing that they had been unable to find more ginkleberries. The commander likely would not have connected them with the prophesy if Shimar was still disguised as a Myrondite.

After breakfast the commander approached the girls, and sitting down upon a large rock, he cleared his throat. "We make plans now."

"How are we going to get into the fortress to rescue anybody?" Shimar wanted to know. Hushem had been annoyingly vague when she had asked him a similar question, but this commander of the clan army was a little more forthcoming. Apparently he had come over to discuss this very thing.

"There is secret way. We know. We too big, too clumsy to use. We show you where. You go. You small and nimble. You clever. You rescue leader. He raise porticos. Let us in." The Commander spoke as if stating a simple fact. Shimar knew it would not be as easy as he made it sound, but she had no better plan to offer, so she said nothing. Taking her silence as agreement the brute rose and began to organize his men. They would set out at once for Salthazar's fortress.

"I don't know why I allow myself to get talked into these things." Shimar shook her head.

"Because deep in your heart you know it is the right thing to do." Melki replied cheerfully as the girls joined the army's march southward.

Kendrig was shocked to hear the milling group of Myrondite slaves yelling for Zebach's execution. Many had followed Zebach around and claimed to be his followers. Just three days ago, they were shouting "Hail to the High King and his son!" and cheering at what he had to say. Now these same ones were calling out for his death. Don't they know who he is? Can't they see how wrong this execution is? Not just because Zebach was innocent of any evil, but because of what he stood for.

Kendrig could not understand it. Zebach had been betrayed by those he loved and trusted. Only a small handful still believed in Zebach, and most of them were in hiding, too scared to come forward lest they be executed too. Kendrig gently fingered the braided ribbon bracelet on his wrist, remembering the words that Zebach had spoken.

What could it all mean? There were plenty of things that he didn't understand, but one thing he was sure of. Zebach was the prince, the son of the High King, and he had come to help the slaves, to uplift those who are oppressed, and set the captives free. How could so many of them now turn against him?

Being in the middle of the angry crowd, Kendrig doubted if he could have gotten away even if he had wanted to. This didn't overly concern him because he had no intention of leaving just then. As painful as this was to witness, he had to find out what was to become of Zebach. Yes, he would stay regardless of the consequences to himself. Just then he felt a hand on his arm, and a gruff voice behind him asked "Hey, aren't you one of his followers?" Kendrig turned around and looked up into the sneering face of a huge Tephanite guard.

"No..... You must be mistaken...." he blurted out in panic.

"I'm sure I saw you with him." The guard insisted "there aren't too many like you in these slave pits. With your blonde hair, blue eyes and fair skin you really stand out amongst all these Myrondites."

"You're Wrong! By the Moons I don't even know the man!" Kendrig swore. Thoroughly unconvinced, the big Tephanite scrutinized the young man carefully. In the uncomfortable silence that followed, Kendrig squirmed under the burly guard's penetrating gaze.

After what seemed an eternity, the Tephanite shrugged his massive shoulders and turned his attention back to what was happening with the condemned prisoner up front. When Kendrig tried to do the same, his eyes met Zebach's deep brown ones. The sorrow he saw there rent his heart in two. It hit him like a crushing weight.

He knows that I denied being his friend! A gasping sob escaped Kendrig's mouth. He had to get out of there right now. As he fled, a path miraculously opened up through the sea of people. He ran his fastest, leaving the crowds behind. All too soon, he came to a dead end. Angrily Kendrig gazed up at the stone walls towering above him.

That was one of the problems with the slave pits. Nowhere to run. He heaved a sigh. What did it matter anyway? No matter how he tried, he could not run from himself and what he had done. He could not escape the memory of the look in Zebach's' eyes. In grief and frustration, he threw himself face down on the ground and wept bitterly.

Shimar gasped out loud, as she looked up at the enormous fortress that towered over the desert sand from a height of more than three hundred feet. It was even larger and more intimidating than she had imagined. How could they possibly get in to free the clan leader without being noticed? The closer they came to the formidable structure, the more hopeless and foolish the plan seemed.

They reached a hollow several hundred yards from the high walls of the fortress. The commander signaled his army to stay there while he went on with the girls. Obediently they crouched down to wait. Shimar wondered what the point of all the sneaking was. Surely, the guards on top of the wall must have already spotted them despite the camouflage of the gray cloaks that they all wore. If they had been sighted there was no indication of it.

Still Shimar felt exposed and vulnerable as she and Melki stealthily followed the commander over the sand dunes. Did the gray cloaks really disguise them? Of course, everything seemed to be gray out here in the forbidden desert. Even the sky was dull and overcast. Oh, how she wished Hushem were still with them. Somehow, his presence seemed to have a calming effect on her. Why did he have to leave just when they needed him the most?

Nordelia wiped the sweat off her forehead with the back of her hand as she leaned on her shovel for a moment to catch her breath. She was both physically and emotionally exhausted. She was past caring. Even when one of the guards stuck her and ordered her to get to work, she just stood staring at him vacantly.

It was as if her heart had withered up and died. She could not get the execution out of her mind. It had been so awful! She didn't want to think about it, but she feared that those sad brown eyes would haunt her the rest of her life. What was there about the man that bothered her so? After all, he was just a

Myrondite slave, wasn't he? She could not understand why Kendrig and Jonkin had been so impressed with him.

Of course, she really knew nothing about the man, having just arrived at the slave pits. She gave a big sigh and went back to her digging. What did it matter now anyway? He was dead now so that was the end of it, wasn't it? Then why couldn't she stop thinking about him? She shook her head in a vain effort to cast off her brooding thoughts.

Nothing really mattered anymore. The slave pits had changed everyone. Even Jonkin was not the carefree, outgoing person that he had been. There was something haunting about his expression. Here they were stuck in the slave pits with no hope of being freed. All was lost, so why bother worrying about it. She just didn't have the energy.

A lonely wind blew across the deserted hillside, bending the tall grass before it. Hushem and the four moon dancers stood staring at the mound of cold ashes inside the ring of stones.

"I don't understand it. They should be here." Hushem shook his head, causing his long white beard to sway form side to side.

"Well they're not!" Cleotisha retorted, "So, now what do we do?"

"Is it just my imagination, or have we been heading back toward the slave pits?" demanded Jerah.

"Yes, as a matter of fact that is precisely where we are going." the old Myrondite told them.

"You're nuts!" Jerah exploded "You tell us that we aren't safe in a Crolarmite village, so you lead us right back into Salthazar's clutches."

"You must understand. Tonight we have the full moons. Events are taking place in the slave pits this day that will shake Ku-Lammorah to its very core. The moon dancers must be there!" Hushem spoke earnestly, his calm brown eyes staring evenly into her angry blue ones.

"Look at all these footprints. Shimar did not make these." Resha timidly spoke up.

Hushem bent down to peer at the marks in the dust that Resha indicated. He straightened up to meet the anxious eyes of the four moon dancers, his own face a mask of concern.

"No she didn't, and neither did Melki." he spoke in a grave tone. "I fear they have been taken by Tephanite soldiers. A large troop of them, by the looks of things." With a sweep of his hand, he indicated flattened grass all around.

Shimar glanced anxiously up at the wall that towered above them. Still no signs that the Tephanite soldiers were aware of their presence. The commander indicated a breech in the wall right where it joined the tower. She could well see why the clan needed them.

There was no way that one of the brutes could squeeze his bulk through that crack. Indeed, it took a great deal of squirming and wiggling for Shimar and Melki to manage it. At last, they stood inside the base of the tower.

Darkness surrounded them like a blanket. They had made it this far but she was not about to relax and let down her guard. As they stood in silence, listening, Shimar couldn't help wondering if they were walking into some kind of trap.

The whole place reeked of fear and death. She heard Melki fumbling in her pack. Soon Shimar found herself squinting against the light of the torch, which seemed amazingly bright in the confined space. They were surrounded by curved stone walls on all sides. The dirt floor was littered with bits of stone that had crumbled away over the years. A very steep, narrow staircase spiraled around the inside wall of the tower. It started near the passage where they had entered. By the time it had circled the enclosure once, it was already at least ten or twelve feet above this crevice in the wall. From there it continued up and up until it disappeared from view.

"Oh my!" Melki gasped as she gazed up into the blackness.

"You can say that again." Shimar agreed in a whisper.

"I wonder why there are no floors in this tower. Usually they are divided into rooms, one on top of the other." Melki muttered.

"It's very ancient. Who knows how long it has been since anyone has been here. Perhaps the floors have collapsed and fallen down." Shimar quietly suggested.

"There would be a lot more rubble if that was so. Besides I don't see any doors at all." Melki held the torch high and they both peered up as far as they could.

She was quite right. There were no doors within sight, or anything else for that matter, to indicate where floors might have been. The only thing that she could see was occasional metal rings embedded in the stone wall. She was not sure what they were for. Possibly the staircase used to have a railing, and this was all that remained. With a shrug of her slender shoulders, Melki began to ascend the narrow stone stairs. Knowing that it was useless to put it off any longer, Shimar followed hesitantly.

Yorg-Dogmah scurried into the throne room and bowed low in front of the dark figure seated up on the dais.

"You...you s-sent for me, my Lord." he mumbled in a voice that was barley audible.

"Relax. I have not summoned you here for punishment." Salthazar assured his cringing henchman.

"But my Lord....." Yorg-Dogmah began.

"True, our plan to flush out the fifth moon dancer has failed, but no matter. She is here. Right here within the walls of the fortress. I can sense her presence."

"You d-don't understand. The....the other moon dancers.... They're gone." The brute stammered, not daring to look up at the imposing figure on the throne.

"Nonsense!" Salthazar hissed. "Ethan has them safe in his village."

"Th-thats what I'm trying to tell you." Yorg-Dogmah spoke hesitantly. "I just had a report from Ethan. A-apparently s-some one... uh.... somebody...."

"Whatever it is you are trying to say, spit it out." the dark lord said impatiently.

"They are gone my Lord. They were spirited away in the middle of the night."

"What!" Salthazar seethed. "Why must I put up with incompetent fools?" Staring down at the quivering mountain of muscle bowed low before him, he ordered, "Don't you realize how vital it is that we have all five moon dancers tonight? Get some men together. Go out and find them immediately!"

"Yes my Lord. I understand...." Yorg-Dogmah said, still prone in front of the dark lord.

"No, I don't think you do. If you did you would be out searching for the moon dancers instead of groveling and sniffling here, wasting my time." Salthazar's voice was quiet but his tone threatening. Yorg-Dogmah scrambled to his feet and backed hastily out of the throne room.

Shimar gulped, trying to swallow her panic, and forced herself to stare straight ahead at Melki's' back. The higher they climbed the more she felt the need of something to hang on to. Oh, where was the next ring in the wall? She knew she did not dare look down, as they made their way slowly up the narrow spiral stairway that ascended the well-like interior of the tower. She would be sure to feel dizzy if she gazed into the black depths beneath them. As it was, She had a difficult time keeping her mind from imagining plunging to her death some three hundred feet below. It didn't help when they came to a place where the stairs had crumbled away.

"There is the next Iron ring. If you can give me a boost I think I can reach it, and pull myself up to where the staircase continues. Then I can reach down and help you up." Melki said as she calmly propped up the torch in the corner of the stair.

"You've got to be kidding!" Shimar exclaimed as she gazed up to where Melki pointed. "You not only have to get enough height but it would mean leaning way forward over nothing in order to reach it. Even if by some miracle you manage to get up there, how do you know that part of the stairs won't crumble away too?"

"Don't be afraid. I'll be hanging onto the iron ring. I'll be all right." Melki said with a confident smile.

"And if the ring pulls out of the wall?" Shimar asked.

"Look, if you have a better idea let's hear it. If not, then boost me up so I can get a hold of that ring." Melki demanded in a cross voice.

Shimar knew it was useless to argue further, so she joined Melki on the last step before the chasm, and laced her fingers together. Melki placed her hands on Shimar's shoulders, and stepped one foot up onto Shimar's' proffered hands.

"It's a good thing you're fairly light or I wouldn't be able to do this." Shimar commented. "Can you reach the ring?"

"Just a little bit further over." Melki informed her.

"Well, if I lean over anymore we'll both plunge to our deaths." Shimar grunted. "and I don't think I can hold you up much longer."

"Well, can you just push me a little further over. Just a couple of inches more and I'll have it." Melki entreated.

"But if you miss the ring, I won't be able to stop you from falling." Shimar argued.

"Just do it!" Melki demanded, as she stretched her hand as far as she could towards the iron ring that lay frustratingly just beyond her reach. Shimar heaved Melki with all her strength.

"I've got it!" Melki crowed triumphantly, as with a great deal of effort, she managed to scramble up onto the stairs. With one hand holding firmly to the ring, she reached the other one down towards where Shimar waited below.

"Are the steps you're on good and solid, or are they threatening to crumble away too?" Shimar asked hesitantly, ashamed to show her fear in the face of Melki's bravery.

"They're fine, but I can't quite reach you. Just a minute. I have an idea." Melki took off her rope belt and tied one end securely to the rope ring. She wrapped the other end around her wrist and hung on tight. Then, kneeling on the edge of the step she was able to lean down and take Shimar's outstretched hand. Taking a firm hold of Shimar's arm, she pulled up with all her strength.

Shimar experienced a moment of shear terror as her feet treaded thin air over the chasm. With the aid of fear induced adrenaline, and Melki pulling her, Shimar too, managed to clamber to the relative safety of the narrow stone stairs. In her panic, she climbed right over top of Melki and lay gasping and panting for air. She clung to the cold stone, reluctant to rise to her feet in spite of the sharp edges of the steps digging into her ribs.

"Come on. Let's go!" Melki's voice came from right behind her, sounding impatient. Shimar forced herself to her feet and they continued their ascent. It grew darker as they left the small flickering light of the torch further and further below.

As it turned out, there was not much further to climb. The stairs just seemed to end with a solid wooden roof above them and no way of continuing. At least, none that they could see in the dim light.

"This is just great! Now what do we do?" Shimar demanded of Melki, her voice rising in panic.

"I don't know. There has to be away. The clan commander said...."

"I know what he said," Shimar snapped. "but what if the secret passage had been boarded over? It's not like the clan have been here recently or anything." Just then, they heard the creak and a groan of rusty hinges as a trap door opened above them. Light from the square opening flooded the stairwell, painfully glaring in the girl's eyes. Squint as they might, their blinded eyes could not make out the features of the large face that peered curiously down at them.

Moon Dancers

☽ ● ☾

Chapter fifteen:

As Shimar's eyes grew accustomed to the light she was able to make out the features of the face that hovered over them. She could tell that it was not one of the Tephanite guards. It had to be the leader of the clan.

"Who are you? Why you come?" he asked, as he reached a huge hairy arm down to help them up through the trapdoor.

"We are friends of the clan. We have come to rescue you. You are the clan leader, aren't you?" Shimar replied, as she stood up in the tower room and dusted herself off.

"It is me.," the clan leader confirmed, thumping his chest with a large knobby finger. "But two young girls rescue me?" He was incredulous. As he thought about it, a grin spread across his big ugly face, and he erupted with a very loud, deep belly laugh.

"But it's true! Your troops are waiting outside the walls to storm the fortress. We really have come to get you out of here." Melki insisted.

"How? Me no can go down same way you come up." the clan leader pointed out. His heavy brow furrowed in thought as he wandered over to where the late afternoon sun poured in the narrow window. He scratched his head as he stared down at the desert below.

"You can't see them, but they are down there." Shimar assured him. "We have to get the porticos raised so they can get in. It's not going to be easy to get past the Tephanite guards but........."

"How we get out of tower?" the hairy brute asked again.

With a triumphant grin, Melki reached inside her tunic, and pulled out the cord that she wore around her neck. Dangling from the end of the cord was the set of keys that she had retrieved by the river. Shimar stared at the large ring of keys and groaned.

"There must be over a hundred of them, and with our luck none of them will work."

With Shimar and the clan leader on her heels, Melki crossed to the door in quick, purposeful strides and began trying the various keys in the lock. She had tried well over half of them before she finally hit upon the correct one. The key turned easily in the lock and the heavy wooden door opened with a protesting creak.

With a sigh of relief, Melki hurried over to the window. Reaching her arm as far as she could, she waved a large red handkerchief as a signal to the troop of clan soldiers waiting below. The Clan leader and the two girls then slipped out the door of the tower room and made their way onto the top of the walls that surrounded the fortress.

"I still can't believe we're doing this!" Jerah muttered under her breath.

"None of us are thrilled to be going back to Lord Salthazar's fortress, but I think it is necessary if we are to fulfill the prophesy." Cleotisha commented. Although she appeared outwardly calm, she could not keep the apprehension out of her voice.

"I'm scared!" Resha's lip trembled.

"Don't be afraid. The High King knows what he is doing. Everything is sure to unfold as it should." Hushem reassured her, as he and the four girls approached the huge stone fortress that loomed three hundred feet above them.

"Why should we trust you? Myrondites don't exactly have a reputation for being trustworthy." Jerah challenged, her voice full of contempt. Her snappy blue eyes looked directly into Hushem's brown ones.

"Shush!" he commanded urgently, placing a restraining hand on her arm. "What is going on? There is movement down in that hollow ahead. It would appear that we are not the only ones just outside Salthazar's lair. Who are they and what are they doing out here?" Concern creased Hushem's dark brow, and he stroked his long beard in concentration.

"There is the signal! We attack now!" the commander of the clan army shouted, with one of his long fingers pointing up at the red banner that waved out the tower window. With whoops and loud roars, the large brutes with their primitive weapons charged over the sand dunes that surrounded Salthazar's fortress.

The brute knew that the only chance of the assault on the slave pits succeeding was for them to raise the porticos. Would the clan leader and the two girls be able to accomplish this? It did not seem likely; however, the commander had great faith in the prophecy. He had no time to ponder further, for the battle had begun.

"How in the name of the Prenellium City are we ever going to make it past the guards up ahead?" Shimar wondered as she, along with Melki and the clan leader, made their way stealthily along the top of the wall, keeping to the shadows as much as possible. Although the ruckus below had captured the attention of the guards, the chances of slipping past them unnoticed were not good. The clan leader obviously had no such qualms. As bold as brass he marched right past the guards.

So intent were the Tephanites on raining arrows down on the clan below that they did not notice what was going on right behind them. Shimar and Melki exchanged looks. Melki shrugged her slender shoulders, then quietly followed the clan leader.

Shimar felt she had little choice, so she hurried to catch up. The two girls silently slipped past, behind the very backs of the burly guards, and joined the clan leader in the small guardroom where the machinery to raise the porticos was located. The giant was already exerting his enormous strength to turn the huge metal crank. With creaks and groans, the huge iron porticos began to rise. The clan army cheered as they surged toward the open gate. The shocked Tephanite guards, up on the wall, let out an angry cry and rushed to the alcove where the clan leader and the two girls were.

"We have got to hide!" Melki's voice was shrill with panic.

Indeed, Shimar could see that their only hope was the slim chance that they could continue to avoid detection. Looking around, they found that the small-enclosed space they were in offered no place to hide. Indeed, the room held little apart from the machinery used to raise and lower the porticos. Shimar began to share Melki's panic as the thudding sound of the guards' footsteps approached. The room had only one door through which the Tephanites were about to enter.

"Quick! Out the window!" the clan leader ordered. Without waiting for them to react, he picked the girls up as if they weighed nothing and plopped them onto a narrow ledge that ran along beside the window. With a great deal of squirming, he managed to heave his bulk through the narrow window and up onto the ledge to join Melki and Shimar. No sooner was he situated then the Tephanites burst into the room.

"Quick! Help me lower the gate! We must stop anymore of those disgusting mutants from getting in." a burly guard called out. After a few minutes of concerted effort, he gave up. "It's no good! The mechanism is jammed somehow." By this time, the entire clan army was in the courtyard below.

"How did it happen? The porticos could not just raise itself." one of the Tephanites commented. The brutes rolled their huge yellow eyes fearfully. Unwilling to stay any longer than necessary where such strange goings-on occurred, they hurried to join the battle before they were blamed for the breach of the fortress. Lord Salthazar would not forgive those he judged responsible for this disaster. They were sure to be tortured unmercifully.

Once the coast was clear, the clan leader squeezed back through the window. Reaching out his muscular arms, he helped the girls climb back inside. Shimar doubted very much if she could have made herself move without his help. She stood for a moment, attempting to quiet her pounding heart. No matter how many times she was forced to face her fear of heights, it did not get any easier.

As they slipped out of the gatehouse, their attention was immediately drawn to the battle taking place below them. The clan was met with a strong resistance. Although the Tephanites had been taken by surprise, now they fought with savage fury and deadly skill. The clan, numbering in the thousands, filled the courtyard. The chill morning air was filled with yelling, the clashing of swords and the din of the battle that raged all around. The sheer numbers of the clan beat the Tephanites back so that Salthazar's soldiers were unable to close the gates again.

Swinging swords, maces and war hammers, the wild brutes engaged the Tephanite soldiers in hand to hand combat. The enormous courtyard was a rolling sea of soldiers as the stormy battle blew first this way and then that. The din was incredible. Battle cries mixed with the screams of the wounded, and the clang of metal weapons rang throughout the slave pits.

"Who are those big hairy brutes? I'm sure they aren't Tephanites." Cleotisha wondered aloud.

"I'm not sure, but we might as well follow them inside, since they so graciously opened the door for us." Hushem quipped, indicating the yawning archway left by the raised porticos. This entrance was guarded on either side by a giant stone statue of a lazigger. Hushem bowed towards the girls, and with a sweep of his hand indicated for them to go first.

"Why is it again, that we are returning to this horrible place?" Resha wanted to know. She shuddered with dread as she gazed up at the evil fortress towering over them.

"Because our rescuer here has some kind of special knowledge from the High King, who indicates that our presence is necessary." Jerah muttered.

"It's going to be okay." Tonnash spoke quietly, as if trying to convince herself.

All four girls started walking towards the entrance to the slave pits. Cleotisha, lost in thought, was being uncharacteristically quiet. Jerah's mouth was set in a grim line. She was obviously none too happy about what they were doing. Resha and Tonnash stared up at the huge stone birds of prey with eyes full of fear. Cleotisha had to admit to feeling a little bit nervous herself as they hesitantly walked between the two statues, Hushem bringing up the rear.

"Something's happening out there!" Nordelia announced as she burst into the barracks where Jonkin, Kendrig, Bretlig and Abiud gathered with a few of Zebach's followers. The sprawling building had no windows, and the only door was the one that Nordelia had just entered. The small group, cowering in the dark shadows, was attempting to lay low in the hopes that they might escape Salthazar's notice, and thus his wrath.

"What are you talking about?" Kendrig grumbled. He was still grieving for his friend and did not wish to be disturbed.

"I think the fortress is under attack. Whatever is happening has thrown the guards into a real tizzy."

"Who would be insane enough to attack Lord Salthazar?" Bretlig asked, but he was already pushing past Nordelia, and hurrying out the door to see for himself what was going on.

"Look! I don't believe it! It's Shimar!" Resha called out, pointing off to the right where Shimar was rapidly descending a stone staircase. She was followed by a big hairy brute, and a slim Myrondite girl, who was madly waving a red handkerchief to get their attention. Shimar reached the bottom of the steps, and rushed over to them. The girls clung to one another desperately. Melki, for her part, was relieved and overjoyed to be reunited with Hushem.

"Come on! We have got to get out of the line of fire." Shimar said emphatically, pointing in the direction that the clan leader had run off to join his men.

"Where will we be safe?" Cleotisha wondered.

"Perhaps that young man knows. He seems to be trying to get our attention." Hushem commented calmly, nodding towards Bretlig who was approaching from the sidelines.

"Bretlig! I might have known I'd find you in the middle of a battle." Jerah called out joyfully as she embraced her brother. Bretlig quickly led the group back to the barracks where they could make plans. Tonight was the night of the full moons. This was not a Crolarmite village but perhaps they could perform the moon dance after all.

At first, it appeared that the clan would prevail through the advantage of sheer numbers as well as the element of surprise. However, gradually the tide of battle began to turn. The superior weapons and training of the Tephanite soldiers drove the clan back into a corner of the massive courtyard. After that, the battle was swift and decisive. Those of the clan army who were not dead or dying were trapped in the slave pits with no way out.

It was not long before their ankles were all encased in shackles, and joined together with thick chains. It was made abundantly clear that any of them who resisted or caused any trouble would be tortured to death. The clan attack on the stone fortress had succeeded only in Lord Salthazar gaining many more slaves. As if to seal their doom, they heard the porticos clammer and clank into place with a fearsome sence of finality.

Shimar noted that Kendrig hardly looked up when she and Bretlig entered, followed by Hushem and the girls. However, a moment later he was among newcomers enthusiastically welcoming his sister Jerah, and the others. In fact, the girls were immediately surrounded by family and friends. There amongst them was the one Shimar most longed to see. Although Jonkin greeted her warmly, embracing her gently, he seemed somewhat distracted and subdued. There was something different about him. Shimar could not put her finger on it. This was not the Jonkin that she knew and felt so close to. She could tell by his appearance that he had been through a lot, but what would change a person so dramatically?

There was much noise and confusion, as everybody tried to talk at once. Eventually everyone was caught up on everyone else's news, and plans began in earnest for the moon dance to be performed that very night, right there in the slave pits. The Crolarmites among the slaves were convinced that this would deal a crippling blow to Salthazar's power. In spite of the danger, at the right time the original five dancers would dance under Ku-lammorah's three moons. Nordelia was not sure whether to feel relieved or envious now that she would no longer be taking Shimar's place.

Hushem and Melki were not sure if doing the moon dance was such a good idea. They sat in a corner, away from the others, saying little. Melki's face was a mask of worry and Hushem's brow was furrowed deep with a frown.

Later when they were all eating their scant ration of food, Hushem spied the medallion around Kendrig's neck.

"You are not a Myrondite so you can't be him! How did you come to possess such an item?" Hushem demanded suspiciously.

"Hey, it's very similar to the medallion that I lost. This one is larger but it had many of the same symbols on it. Where did you get it?" Melki exclaimed as she leaned closer to peer at the artifact.

"A friend gave it to me for safe keeping, the Myrondite I told you about, the one they executed this morning…. He said to keep it hidden inside my shirt. I didn't even do that right." Kendrig's voice broke as he choked back a sob.

"Could it possibly have been him? What does it all mean?" Hushem muttered to himself under his breath. He then grew quiet, lost in thought.

"He's gone! Someone has taken his body!" Nordelia breathlessly rushed up to Kendrig.

"Calm down and tell me what happened." Kendrig leaned on his shovel and gave the frightened girl his full attention.

"I went to take Zebach some flowers and the door to the tomb was open. The guards that Salthazar posted there were gone and so was his body. Who would have taken him? Where could they have put him?" Nordelia spoke quickly, almost frantically.

"But that's impossible!" Kendrig sputtered.

"Go and see for yourself if you don't believe me.," she told him.

The guards had seemed rather distracted ever since the attack by the clan, so Kendrig did not hesitate. He dropped his shovel and rushed off to the stone crypt without another word.

Moon Dancers

$$\text{)} \bullet \text{(}$$

Chapter sixteen:

The courtyard of Salthazar's fortress was hushed and still. It was almost as if the whole land of Ku-Lammorah was holding its breath. The pale silvery light of the full moons gave the five figures a ghostly appearance. The long gowns swirled gently as the five girls began to circle slowly, gradually picking up speed as they dipped and twirled gracefully. With perfect synchronization, they performed the beautiful flowing movements of the moon dance.

"No!" Salthazar screamed in fury, shattering the silence. "Stop the dance at once or you die! Archers ready your bows." However, the Archers were frozen like statues, so enchanted were they by the lithe, willowy movements of the moon dancers. Salthazar continued to rant and rave with growing panic, but no one paid any attention. All eyes were focused on the dance.

Once the dark Lord realized that his commands were not bringing results, he too, fell quiet. The silence became heavy and oppressive. The only ones moving were the dancers. The five girls completed their dance. Salthazar's red eyes darted furtively back and forth, as if expecting danger from some unknown quarter. Then all was stillness.

Even the moon dancers had now become like statues in the ghostly moonlight. Despite the crowd on the sidelines, the courtyard felt empty and desolate, as if no living soul had been there in eons. Finally, a smug grin began to creep onto Salthazar's evil countenance.

"So the prophecy has failed. I was a fool to think that five girls dancing would be any kind of threat. I have won! The so-called High King has lost! Guards, execute the moon dancers." The silence that followed his words was deafening. No one moved. An eternity passed. Finally, the dark Lord tore the stillness apart.

"You heard me! I said execute them!" Salthazar ordered from his position on the top step, just in front of the entrance to his palace.

Thick black clouds blotted out much of the silvery light of the full moons. A cold wind whistled through the courtyard. The Tephanite soldiers stood frozen on the spot. In the limited light, they resembled grey stone statues of giant ogres or trolls. Almost as one, they shook themselves as if to break the spell. They then swiftly took the five girls into custody.

"Yes, the five lovely girls will make a suitable sacrifice." he mused. He rubbed his hands together in glee. Turning to the moon dancers, he gloated. "So, you thought you could defeat me, did you? Ha! No one is a match for me."

"Do you desire the execution to take place tonight my Lord?" one of the guards politely inquired.

"Of course tonight, you imbecile! Burn them at the stake at once." The dark lord's piercing red eyes glared at those nearest him. Immediately the Tephanites scurried off, almost bumping into one another in their haste to do Salthazar's bidding.

"I can't believe he would do this! After all the faithful service I've given him." Draklog pounded his fist into his open palm in frustration.

"It's terrible of course, but since we can't do anything about it, it is best if we don't make waves." Eliphaz wagged his chin back and forth and patted Draklog's' arm in a phony show of sympathy.

"This is my daughter we are talking about! If you expect me to sit idly by while they execute her and the other dancers you are crazy!" Draklog exploded, his face growing redder than his hair.

"Shush! Keep your voice down. Surely, you are not going to confront Lord Salthazar. That would be suicide." warned Eliphaz, looking nervously around to see if they had attracted any notice. The guards seemed to all be occupied preparing the five pyres. Draklog pounded his fist into the wall, and paced back and forth in the corner of the courtyard, mumbling incoherently to himself.

The moon dancers were tied tightly to wooden stakes in the center of the courtyard. Silence fell over the crowd that was gathered. The only sound or movement was a slight rustling of the wind through the dry twigs and leaves that were heaped up all around the five girls. A burly Tephanite guard stood at each pyre, torch in hand, waiting for the signal from Salthazar to light the pyre.

"Well, now do you admit that I have won?" Salthazar gloated, a triumphant grin on his hideous face.

The flickering light of the torches held by the guards were reflected in the glowing red eyes of the dark Lord. Just as Salthazar was about to raise his long thin arm to signal the guards to proceed, Kendrig forced his way through the crowd.

"No! Stop! You can't do this!" he shouted

"Who would dare to tell me what I can and can't do?" Salthazar sneered as he gazed down with contempt at the young man before him.

Then the dark Lord's eyes fell on the medallion that hung around Kendrig's neck. Since Zebach's execution, Kendrig had spent much time fingering the shiny disc, and pondering its meaning. Unfortunately, he too often forgot to tuck it safely out of sight inside his shirt.

"What is that around your neck? You can't be the one. You're a Crolarmite. Who gave it to you? Tell me at once." Salthazar demanded, taking a step back.

"Zebach." Kendrig answered, boldly stepping closer. He held the medallion out towards Salthazar as far as the chain would allow without removing it from around his neck.

"Fool! Do you really think I fear that insignificant amulet?" the dark Lord taunted.

"Perhaps not, but you do fear the High King, don't you" Kendrig commented.

"You are nothing but a worm. How dare you talk to me in such a manner." Salthazar seethed. He paused, his red eyes boring into Kendrig as if trying to discover the source of such unmitigated gall. When he spoke, his voice was quiet, but even more menacing. "The blonde dancer is your sister, is she not? You shall share her fate as well as her stake." Turning to the guards, he commanded, "Tie him up quickly! Let's get on with this."

"That's right! Hurry up before the High King stops you. He will put an end to your evil, you know. Your days are numbered. You won't rule much longer." Kendrig didn't know where these words came from. They just popped into his head and he couldn't resist saying them. He knew it was useless to struggle so he did not waste his energy as two hulking guards took him in their vise-like grip. They led him to the stake where Jerah was tied. Using strong rope, they bound him to the other side of the pole so that brother and sister were fastened securely back to back.

All was in readiness. At Salthazar's signal, the pyres were lit. The fires crackled to life, illuminating the pale faces of the dancers as well as many of those in the crowd gathered in the courtyard. Indeed, the faces of some of the spectators showed more anguish than those of the five dancers.

"You will not do this!" commanded a voice full of authority.

"Who dares order me? Show yourself at once!" Salthazar was incredulous.

A figure stepped out of the shadows, and walked right up to the dark Lord. Pulling back the hood of his cloak to reveal his face he announced. "I am Zebach." There were loud gasps from the crowd.

"How can this be? I had you put to death." Salthazar's long thin hand flew to his throat. He shrank back, visibly shaken.

"I have conquered death. Therefore I declare that these young people shall not die." Zebach looked up and raised his hands towards the night sky. It immediately started to pour down rain. The deluge lasted only a few moments but it was sufficient to put out the flames that surrounded the feet of the dancers.

Zebach beaconed Kendrig and the girls to come to him. To every ones utter amazement they were able to do this without delay or hindrance. The ropes that had bound them were completely burned away, yet the six young people were completely unharmed. The crowd erupted into cheers. Even some of the Tephanite guards were rejoicing. Those that weren't were staring opened mouthed in stunned silence.

"Where did Salthazar go? I'm sure he is up to no good." Nordelia asked, peering into the shadows.

"Who knows? He must have slipped away during the rain." Bretlig shrugged his shoulders.

"Come. Join us, daughter." Zebach beaconed Nordelia over.

She trembled as she approached with downcast eyes. When she reached the other dancers, she glanced up to find Zebach gazing intently down at her. His deep brown eyes seemed to search her very soul.

"Are you willing to trust me?" he asked

"Yes." Nordelia's voice, choked with emotion, was barely above a whisper.

A few of the Tephanite guards approached the Prince, and bowed prostrate at his feet. Whispers and murmurs rippled through the crowd.

"Welcome sons of stone, sons of thunder. The High King delights to have such as you become his followers." Zebach smiled warmly and gently helped the brutes to their feet.

"You would befriend our enemies? How can you betray our people this way?" an angry voice cried out. Much grumbling among the Myrondite slaves indicated that the man was not alone in his sentiments.

"None are my enemies who serve my father. True, these men have not always done so. Today they made a difficult choice, and they will be accepted. Those forgiven the most, love the most. Those of great repentance can be of great service." With a sweep of his hand, Zebach indicated the tears flowing down the faces of the guards.

"My father invites all to follow him, whether they are Myrondite, Crolarmite, Tephanite or clan. All will be accepted who seek my father with a pure heart." Zebach's gentle voice echoed powerfully across the stillness of the courtyard. He turned to address the moon dancers.

"Daughters of the night." Zebach's deep voice echoed across the courtyard as he spoke to the moon dancers. "On this day you have been set free! You have now become daughters of light. No longer will you follow the moons. From this day forward, you are to follow the Son. It is almost time to leave this evil place, but first we shall eat. We will need strength. The journey ahead is a long and difficult one."

Torches were lit, and food was brought. There was much feasting and celebration. No one seemed to know, or care very much, where Salthazar and the rest of the guards had gone. Kendrig stood in the shadows, apart from the crowd, watching the proceedings. He ate nothing. His heart filled with dread as Zebach approached him.

"Come friend, have some food. Join the party." The Prince invited with a warm smile.

"I can't! You know what I did. I am not worthy to serve the High King, or to be called your friend. I am weak. When it came to choices, I denied I even knew you." Kendrig's' voice was full of bitterness and self-reproach. His head was hung in shame, and he could not look Zebach in the eye. Tenderly Zebach cupped Kendrig's chin in his hand, and lifted it. Kendrig was forced to meet the gaze of the searching brown eyes. He could not believe the love and compassion that he saw there.

"Do you love me?" Zebach asked quietly and seriously.

"You know my heart. You know what our friendship means to me." There was a catch in Kendrig's' voice as he spoke. The tears that had been glistening in his eyes spilled down his cheeks.

"Is not what I said of the Tephanites just as true of you? My father can use people who have a broken and repentant heart. You say you are weak. I say when you are weak then you are strong. If you trust your own strength then you will fail. If instead, you let your weakness remind you of your need for my Father's strength, the victory is assured." Zebach told him.

"But, how can I be forgiven?" Kendrig shook his head at what he felt was impossible.

"Do you still not understand? That is why I died. Not just to set captives free from slavery, but from guilt as well. I have paid the price in full for all the wrongs ever committed against my father and I. The forgiveness is yours as a free gift. All you have to do is receive it."

When the Prince uttered these words, Kendrig fell to his knees, clung to Zebach's robe, and wept. Gently Zebach raised the young Crolarmite to his feet. Putting his arm around Kendrig's' shoulder, he led him over to where the crowd was gathered around the tables of food.

The first rosy fingers of dawn crept up the eastern horizon. Zebach marched purposefully up to the huge iron gates. He stretched his arms skyward, his face turned upward and expectant in the glow of the rising sun. The ground began to tremble. With many creaks and groans, the porticos rose right to the top. Then all was still. He turned to the crowd who stood with eyes wide in wonder. Some mouths gaped open, while some rubbed their fists in their eyes, as if they could not believe what they saw.

"Come, it is time to venture forth into the light, into freedom." Zebach beckoned as he led the way. Melki happily joined the throng of Myrondite slaves who were singing joyfully as they marched through the huge gateway on their way out of the Salthazar's fortress.

Not all the Myrondite slaves chose to leave the slave pits. Some decided to stay because of old hatreds for other races. Some did not trust Zebach and others stayed due to fear of Salthazar. It is unfortunate but you can't force liberty on anyone. Still, it was a great multitude that clambered over the sand dunes to freedom.

The crowd was made up of both Myrondites and Crolarmites. There were even a few Tephanites and some members of the clan. Of course, there were the moon dancers as well as Melki, the friend and companion that Shimar had shared so much with. There was Nordelia, her brother Abiud, Jerah's two brothers Kendrig and Bretlig and even old Greplog who looked more like his old self then he had since his arrival at the slave pits.

"So, the prophesies have come true after all, although not quite the way we thought." Hushem commented as he stepped up beside Melki and Shimar.

" I never would have thought that the promised deliverer would be the Prince himself. Just think, he actually came down from the Prenellium city to rescue us." Melki's brown eyes glowed as she spoke of Zebach.

"I believe that Zebach said he has a job for us all before we get to go to that wonderful city." Hushem reminded them. "I have a feeling that we are in for some more adventures."

"Yes, undoubtedly they will involve shaky rope ladders, climbing up inside crumbling towers, and perching on narrow window sills that are three hundred feet above the ground. I know how much Shimar loves that kind of thing." Melki teased her friend with a grin.

"You are impossible!" Shimar exclaimed, giving Melki a playful punch in the shoulder.

Ethan clambered over rocks covered with barnacles and seaweed, as he made his way north along the shores of the Zicktel Sea. The salty sea spray dampened his clothing as well as his long dark hair, making it appear even more stringy than usual. He was exhausted, chilled and decidedly uncomfortable. The footing was treacherous and the going difficult. The phosphorescent brineconc seaweed made the rocks slippery but at least they gave a little light on this dark night.

His cold blue eyes glanced furtively around, although he was sure that there was no one on this deserted sea coast for miles in either direction. It would seem that he had successfully escaped Salthazar's wrath, at least for the time being. He still had no idea what had gone wrong. He didn't think the moon dancers suspected him. He had been careful not to let the escape seem too easy. Who had tipped them off? Or had they been abducted from under his very nose? Who would have done such a thing, and why? It was all too much to think about. Right now, he must concentrate on his journey.

Ethan had no definite plans. He just wanted to make it to one of the isolated fishing villages up north. There he would hide out until an opportunity presented itself to work his way back into Lord Salthazar's good graces. His jaw set with grim determination. Somehow, he would find a way. He pressed on along the wild desolate sea coast. The only sound apart from the pounding surf was the lonely, haunting cry of the sea birds.

No torches were lit to relieve the smothering darkness of Salthazar's inner sanctum. He sat in the blackness, motionless on his throne like a carved statue. The dark Lord's brooding was interrupted by a slight shuffling sound, followed by a muffled cough. Salthazar's piercing red eyes probed the shadows in a vain attempt to locate the origin of the offending sound.

"Who's there? Step forward at once and identify yourself!" he demanded.

"It's only me. Sorry to disturb you, my Lord." Draklog mumbled a hasty apology as he approached the throne.

"Well? What do you want?" Salthazar inquired condescendingly.

"It's all the slaves that left….." Draklog began.

"Yes. Yes. What about them?" the dark Lord interrupted impatiently.

"I…ah…I wish to go after them, my Lord and bring them back." The big Crolarmite spoke hesitantly.

"Exactly how do you plan to accomplish this?" Salthazar asked with a sneer.

"Such a large group would not be able to travel very fast. They could not have gotten very far. With your permission, my Lord, I would like to take a troop of your soldiers with me. I'm sure we could easily overtake them." Draklog blurted out. He peered through the dimness at the black-robed figure on the throne, in an attempt to gage the dark Lord's reaction.

"Very well. do as you have suggested. Send Yorg-Dogmah to me, and I will authorize the expedition." Salthazar sounded almost bored as he dismissed Draklog with a wave of his boney hand.

After Draklog's footsteps had died away, the dark lord stroked his chin thoughtfully. "So it has come to this. More than half my slaves gone, and my kingdom in chaos. Well, I may have lost the battle but I will win the war. Zebach puts far too much faith in those weak followers of his. They will be his downfall." Salthazar's red eyes narrowed to slits. The expression on his skeletal face was one of grim determination. "The land of Ku-lammorah will all be mine! Oh this is far from over…..far, far from over."

His grotesque features contorted as he threw back his head. From the core of his being he coughed up a spasm of maniacal laughter. The very chamber shook to its foundations. Those unfortunate enough to be in atttendence were filled with an icy dread. Scewing their eyes shut in terror, they wished for the end of the world.

Glossary of Plants and animals:

Balog – A large shaggy herbavore with wide nostrils and long sharp horns. Their thick course hair is usually rust red in color and they are hunted for their meat.

Brineconc – A pale green seaweed that glows in the dark. It is abundant along the shores of the zicktal sea and used in special lamps to light homes

Cordea – A large white bird with a bright creast of yellow fethers on the top of its head. It is concidered good luck to see one. The Myrondites consider them sacred.

Daulph – A small six legged herbavore with two pronged antlers and a spotted yellow/green hide. They have dainty hooves and are incredibly swift. This is vital for their survival due to fact that they are the favorite food of many preditors.

Ginkle berry bush – This low tree like bush has many small, dark green, heart shaped leaves. The small round yellow blossoms appear in the spring, followed in the summer and early fall by big juicy purple berries. These are wonderful in pies, and make the very best jams and wines.

Gumphalus tree – A large deciduous tree with wide spreading brnaches and large round shiney yellow leaves.

Kalup – A small ugly bird who has the most beautiful song ever heard. It feeds on the necter of native flowers.

Kinjo – A middlesized wolflike carnivore with a sharp horn on its nose and pointy spikes along its spine. It's coat of corse hair is ussly yellow, orange or moss green. They are nocturnal and hunt in packs.

Lazigger – a huge bird of prey with dark grey plumage. They have a large hooked beak and a wingspan of 25-30 feet. It has even been known to carry away young balog in it's powerful talans. It's cry as it attacks is said to paralize it's prey.

List of charactors:

Abiud – Nordelia's shy, older brother. A slim teenage boy with smooth brown hair

Bretlig – Jerah's impulsive twelve year-old brother. A husky, solid built boy who does not look feminine in spite of his blonde curls and blue eyes.

Cheran – Resha's chubby baby brother

Cleotisha – one of the five moon dancers. A big fifteen-year-old with a wild mane of red hair.

Draklog – Cleotisha's father. A big bear of a man with a nasty disposition. A supporter of Lord Sathazar.

Eliphaz – Draklog's sidekick. An unpleasant little man who thinks too highly of himself.

Ethan – A thin pimply teenager. He is from a different crolamite village than the moon dancers.

Greplog – One of the ten village elders. A wise but eccentric old man.

Hannoch – The father of Jerah and her brothers; Bretlig and Kendrig. A highly respected man in the village

Hushem – An elderly Myrondite prophet

Ishbach – Draklog's eldest son. A strong but arrogant young man.

Jerah – One of the moon dancers. A petite fifteen-year-old with blonde curls and blue eyes.

Jonkin – Shimar's boyfriend. A pleasant looking young man with sandy blonde hair and freckles

Kendrig – Jerah's older brother. A strongly built young man with a square jaw, and broad chest. He has a manly appearance in spite of his blonde curls and blue eyes.

Linkot – Cleotisha's brother. Draklog's youngest son.

Lithriss – Hannoch's wife. Mother of Jerah and her brothers.

Melki – A teenage Myrondite girl with dark hair, and laughing brown eyes. She becomes a friend of Shimar's.

Mibzar – One of the ten village elders. Grandfather to Resha and her baby brother Cheran.

Nordelia – Resha's friend. A shy, petite, thirteen year-old with sandy blond hair and freckles.

Pakstig – Tonnash's older brother

Perzac – Cleotisha's brother. Draklog's middle son

Resha – Nordelia's friend, and the youngest moon dancer. A dainty fourteen year-old with thick chestnut curls.

Salthazar – The dark Lord who rules from the slave pits in the forbidden desert.

Shimar – The oldest moondancer. A tal slim teenager with smooth dark hair and blue eyes.

Tonnash – One of the moon dancers. A petite girl with long dark curls

Urilos – Tonnash's father. A burly, bald fisherman.

Wenoch – Cleotisha's Grandmother. Draklog's mother in law. The village medicene woman.

Yorg-Dogmah – A high ranking tephanite officer in Lord Salthazar's army.

Zebach – A Myrondite slave in the slave pits who some beleive is trying to start a revolt against Salthazar. Has a small group of close followers.